J. A. WHITE

SHADOW SCHOOL

DEHAUNTING

 KATHERINE TEGEN BOOKS
An Imprint of HarperCollins Publishers

Katherine Tegen Books is an imprint of HarperCollins Publishers.

Shadow School #2: Dehaunting
Copyright © 2020 by J. A. White

Library of Congress Cataloging-in-Publication Data

Names: White, J. A., author.
Title: Dehaunting / J. A. White.
Description: First edition. | New York, NY : Katherine Tegen Books, an imprint of
HarperCollinsPublishers, [2020] | Series: Shadow school; 2 | Audience: Ages 8–12.
| Audience: Grades 4–6. | Summary: "Cordelia and her friends discover a way to
get rid of all the ghosts that haunt their school–but dehaunting turns out to be more
complicated and dangerous than any of them considered"– Provided by publisher.
Identifiers: LCCN 2020000848 | ISBN 9780062838308 (hardcover)
Subjects: CYAC: Middle schools–Fiction. | Schools–Fiction. | Ghosts–Fiction. |
Haunted places–Fiction.
Classification: LCC PZ7.W58327 Deh 2020 | DDC [Fic]–dc23
LC record available at https://lccn.loc.gov/2020000848

Typography by Andrea Vandergrift
20 21 22 23 24   PC/LSCH   10 9 8 7 6 5 4 3 2 1
❖
First Edition

SHADOW SCHOOL

DEHAUNTING

Also by J. A. White

Nightbooks

The Thickety Series
A Path Begins
The Whispering Trees
Well of Witches
The Last Spell

Shadow School Series
Archimancy
Dehaunting
Phantoms

For the teachers and students
of Ridgewood Avenue School

CONTENTS

1

Ghost Race

Aman stood in the corner of Ms. Dalton's social studies classroom. He looked slightly confused, like a visiting parent who had gotten lost. If you didn't know any better, you would have thought he was alive.

Cordelia Liu knew better.

She stepped closer, examining every inch of the ghost. Her gaze was steady, her breathing unhurried. Any other twelve-year-old would have run screaming, but Cordelia knew much of the lingering dead and found nothing here to frighten her. She calmly noted the tags from a dozen ski slopes dangling from the man's winter coat, the chapped skin of his windburned cheeks, his woolen hat. After learning what she could from the man's appearance, Cordelia slid into a chair in order to observe his actions. The ghost paid her no heed, focusing instead on a point far in the distance, perhaps seeing a world invisible to living eyes. After a few moments, he squinted and raised one gloved hand to his forehead, as though fighting the glare of the sun. Since the curtained windows permitted only a trickle of light into the room, Cordelia knew that the ghost wasn't actually having trouble seeing. He was trying to tell her something.

"Ski goggles," Cordelia said.

She slung her backpack off her shoulders and began rifling through its contents. The only way to free a ghost trapped within the walls of Shadow School was by delivering its Brightkey, which was an object that had been of special significance to the deceased. Since ghosts couldn't talk, Cordelia had to rely on the clues provided by their appearance and actions. Often these clues were difficult to decipher, but sometimes, as with the man before her, the answer was obvious.

"Goggles, goggles," she muttered, digging past the other potential Brightkeys she had grabbed from their new storage room: colorful silk scarves, a battered copy of *David Copperfield*, three double-A batteries. "I know they're here somewhere. . . ."

She paused to flick the sweat from her brow. Usually the interior of Shadow School was as cool as a crypt, but the temperature had been hovering in the low nineties all week–a virtual heat wave for New Hampshire–and Cordelia's tank top was soaked with sweat. The ghost, of course, didn't seem to notice the heat at all.

"Yes!" Cordelia exclaimed, spotting the ski goggles at the bottom of her bag. She yanked them out and checked the time on her phone: 11:58. *Two minutes to go,* she thought. The ghost stared at the goggles dangling from her hand, confused, then bent his knees and swiveled his hips from side to side.

"You like to ski," Cordelia said. "I'm on it. Promise. I'd give you these goggles right now, but I'm having this race with my friends to see who can rescue the most ghosts in an hour, and we're not supposed to start until noon on the dot. Kinda silly, I know, but it was the only way to get my friend Benji to come help. He's been sitting in his house playing video games since the beginning of summer."

Her phone dinged. "Here's Lazybones now," Cordelia said. Benji Núñez had sent her a text:

You ready to go down, Liu?

Please, Cordelia texted back. Unlike u I have a plan.

I don't need a plan. I have SKILLZ.

Maybe at soccer but I'm the GHOST MASTER.

We'll see about that. I'm sending 8 spooks home. At least.

In an hour???? Nope

Watch me

U won't top 5

Still be more than you!

A tiny photo of a platypus wearing a lab coat appeared as Agnes Matheson, the third member of their group, joined the chat.

It's adorable the way you two are fighting over second place. You both know I'm going to win, right?

Check out Ag with the trash talk! replied Benji. We've taught her well.

So proud, added Cordelia.

I'm just happy that I can finally see them, replied Agnes, which prompted a flurry of smiley-face emojis from both her friends. The students and teachers of Shadow School were oblivious to the spirits that roamed its halls; to the best of Cordelia's knowledge, only she, Benji, and Dr. Roqueni, the school's principal, had the natural ability to see them. This had initially created some tension with Agnes, who'd felt like an outsider since the spirits remained invisible to her. Fortunately, she had discovered a special pair of goggles that allowed her to see them, and now the three friends were on equal footing. Cordelia suspected that helping the ghosts would be much easier from now on—and a lot more fun.

The clock on her phone changed to 12:00.

GAME TIME!!!!!!!!!!!!!!!!!!!!!!!! Benji texted.

Cordelia didn't reply. Instead, she slid the ski goggles across the floor, expecting the ghost to eagerly snatch them up.

He ignored them.

"Come on, Casper," Cordelia muttered, zipping up her backpack. "I haven't got all day."

She couldn't leave without visual confirmation that the ghost had been freed—otherwise it wouldn't count toward her score. The clock was ticking, however, and she wanted to make sure she snagged some of the easier ghosts before Benji or Agnes got to them first.

Her phone dinged.

One down! Benji texted. The woman staring at that creepy glass carousel. Ticket to an amusement park. This text was followed almost immediately by one from Agnes: Wet guy! Umbrella!

"You're killing me here!" Cordelia told the skier. Then, realizing what she had said, added, "Sorry."

At last, the ghost's eyes settled on the goggles. Cordelia felt her shoulders tense as he leaned forward to pick them up. If they weren't his Brightkey, his hand would pass right through them.

The moment of truth, she thought, biting her lower lip.

The ghost lifted the goggles with ease.

"Boom!" Cordelia exclaimed.

Above the skier, a black triangle appeared. As the entrance to the portal slid open, swirling snowflakes descended from the man's Bright, vanishing the moment they touched the floor. From the world beyond the triangle, Cordelia heard the swish of skiers speeding down a slope, the grinding gears of a lift, laughter. The ghost smiled with delight and rose toward the portal. He pulled the goggles on—they were a little loose, but Cordelia had learned that such details usually didn't matter—and raised his hands into the air, eager for the ski poles that would no doubt be awaiting him on the other side. Cordelia forgot about the hurry she was in and watched in fascination. The sight of a ghost being freed from Shadow School and transported to its own personal paradise never failed to fill her with awe.

Her phone dinged again. Benji.

Jogger. Shoelaces. THAT'S TWO!

Cordelia grunted. The jogger, a new arrival who spent her days stretching outside Mr. Terpin's math class, had been her next stop. Cordelia had been planning to try a pair of earbuds first, but she had also brought shoelaces just in case. A mystifying number of ghosts wanted to spend their afterlife jogging, and it was inevitably one or the other.

Skier, Cordelia texted, already moving. Goggles. Just

getting warmed up.

She broke into a run, navigating the labyrinthine halls of Shadow School with practiced ease. Cordelia would be okay if Agnes beat her—well, sort of okay—but not if Benji did. *I'll never hear the end of it*, she thought, sprinting past boxes of classroom supplies waiting to be unpacked and silent, summer-clean classrooms: chairs stacked, chalkboards scrubbed, sharpeners emptied. The school, for all intents and purposes, was in a state of hibernation until the students returned in six weeks.

Asleep, Cordelia thought, but not empty. *Shadow School is never empty.*

After her slow start with the skier, Cordelia found her rhythm and freed three more ghosts: a girl with a cool punk vibe chilling in room 222 (spiked leather bracelet); a businessman who looked inconvenienced by his demise, as though missing out on a few big deals were the worst of his problems (yesterday's *Wall Street Journal*); and a gamer dude wearing a *Pac-Man* T-shirt whose Bright exploded with the sounds of an eternal arcade (handful of quarters). Unfortunately, not every Brightkey was as easy to identify. A boy wearing a baseball cap had no interest in mitt or ball. In the teachers' room, a stern-looking old man wearing gardening gloves turned his nose at the trowel Cordelia laid at his feet.

Still, with ten minutes remaining until the end of

the race, Cordelia could practically taste victory. She had freed two more ghosts than Agnes, who insisted on immediately cataloging each emancipated spirit in her database before she forgot the "relevant details," and remained only a single ghost behind Benji.

I can do this, Cordelia thought.

She paused to consider her next step. There were a couple of spirits nearby—a redheaded boy holding a wicker basket and a woman wearing a black bridal veil—but Cordelia wasn't very confident about the Brightkeys she had brought for them. What if she had guessed wrong? Trying to help them might be a total waste of time. On the other hand, she was fairly certain about the Brightkeys that would free the two ghosts haunting the attic—but she'd have to cross the entire school to get there, wasting precious minutes.

Take a chance? she wondered. *Or go for the sure thing?*

Cordelia headed toward the attic.

2

Halloween in July

Cordelia burst into the third-floor storage closet and pulled a hidden lever. A panel in the wainscoting clicked open, providing entrance to a dark, narrow passage that inclined toward the upper reaches of the school. Instead of rusting pipes and moldy insulation, as one might find in the innards of normal buildings, the bays framed elaborate wooden designs that resembled spiderwebs. Above Cordelia's head, copper wire linked a series of hollow black pyramids that stood like power stanchions. These pyramids could also be found in a similar passageway that started in the boiler room and coiled around the chimney like a snake.

Their purpose remained one of the many mysteries of Shadow School.

But not for long, Cordelia thought. *Now that we've found Elijah Shadow's office, it's only a matter of time before we unlock all of his secrets.*

With the help of her trusty flashlight, Cordelia navigated the narrow passageway to a trapdoor that led into the attic. Beneath the slanted ceiling, rows of architectural models sat on wooden pedestals like an exhibit of dollhouses. The models ranged from lavish mansions to humble cabins. Each of them was the tiny twin of a house that had once existed in the real world.

Not a normal house. A haunted house.

Elijah Shadow, for whom Cordelia's school was named, had been a brilliant architect and an expert on ghosts. Unlike other authorities on the paranormal, however, he didn't believe that ghosts remained among the living because they were angry or restless. Instead, Elijah had theorized that certain houses were more hauntable than others due to specific architectural characteristics. He used this idea—which he called *archimancy*—to build the ultimate haunted house. Elijah lived there for the rest of his life, studying its spectral inhabitants, and many years after his death, the house became Shadow School.

As Cordelia could attest from firsthand experience,

it was just as haunted now as it had been when Elijah had called it home.

Cordelia climbed the ladder and closed the trapdoor behind her. She was relieved to see that Benji hadn't beaten her to the two ghosts haunting the attic: a little girl wearing a witch mask and carrying a plastic pumpkin, and an old man sitting on a chest, tapping his foot soundlessly against the floor.

She checked her phone.

Five minutes left, she thought. *More than enough time to free both of them.*

Cordelia decided to start with the trick-or-treater. After a solid minute of digging through her stuffed backpack, she finally managed to excavate a handful of soft miniature chocolates.

"Hey there," she said, kneeling so that she was eye level with the girl. She gently placed the chocolates in front of her. "These are for you. They're a little melty. Sorry about that."

The girl didn't seem to mind. She leaned forward, cobalt blue eyes widening behind the holes of her mask, and reached toward the chocolates. The neon light from the glow stick wrapped around her wrist grew in intensity.

Just as the ghost was about to touch the candy, Benji popped his head through the trapdoor. "Wait!" he exclaimed, taking stock of the situation as he scrambled into the attic. He hadn't gotten a haircut all summer, and his long, wavy hair flopped over his eyes. "You don't want those pathetic little things! I have the real deal!"

Benji produced a full-sized Hershey bar from a side pocket of his schoolbag and placed it on the floor. The trick-or-treater peeked over her shoulder and considered this new offering.

"Seriously?" Cordelia asked. "You're going to try to steal my ghost?"

"Don't blame me," Benji replied with an innocent shrug. "It was your idea to turn this into a competition."

"That was the only way I could get you to come! Ever since summer started, it's like you've totally forgotten about the ghosts."

Benji nodded. "It's called a vacation, Cord. You should give it a try."

The trick-or-treater took a few steps in Benji's direction, already reaching for the Hershey bar. "Good choice!" Benji said with a triumphant grin. Usually Cordelia liked his smile, but this one only served to annoy her further. *How can he act like he's better at rescuing ghosts than me when I had to make up this stupid game to get him here in the first place?* She was angry, no doubt about that, but also hurt that she'd had to work so hard to convince him. Even if Benji didn't care about the ghosts, hadn't he wanted to see her?

Cordelia pulled out a handful of chocolates, determined not to let him win. "One measly chocolate bar?" she asked the ghost. "Is that all he's got? I have four different flavors over here!"

The little girl turned to face Cordelia again and cocked her head to one side.

"Are those itsy-bitsy chocolates melted?" Benji asked. Cordelia was gratified to see that the grin had vanished from his face. "I kept mine in a freezer all night. Right now it's perfect."

"I have more!" Cordelia exclaimed, digging out new pieces of candy from the bottom of her bag. "Mr. Goodbar! Tootsie Roll!"

"Nobody likes Tootsie Rolls," Benji said. "Not even ghosts." He unwrapped a corner of the Hershey bar. "Here, I'll get this started for you."

The trick-or-treater turned from Benji to Cordelia, then back to Benji again. The plastic pumpkin shook in her trembling hand. *She's getting frustrated*, Cordelia thought. It wasn't the first time she had seen something like this happen. Sometimes ghosts got upset when she offered them too many incorrect Brightkeys.

That had always been an accident, though, Cordelia thought as the ghost spun back and forth indecisively. *This is completely different. We're teasing this poor girl.*

"We have to stop," Cordelia said, her cheeks warm with shame. "This is mean."

Benji, looking guilty, nodded in agreement. "We're sorry," he told the ghost. "Take any chocolate you want."

"Or take them all," Cordelia added. "The important thing is that you go into your—"

The neon bracelet wrapped around the ghost's wrist exploded in a blinding flash of green. Cordelia shielded her eyes and turned away. When she looked back again, the trick-or-treater was almost upon her: floating, arms outstretched, the tips of her black boots barely touching the floor. Spirits couldn't make physical contact with anything other than their Brightkeys and normally passed through the living with no ill effect. That changed when they were upset. They still couldn't touch the living, but the passage of their fingers through skin and bone left behind a cold, numbing sensation. Cordelia had been "stung" in this way a handful of times. The feeling passed in a few hours, but that didn't mean the ghosts weren't dangerous. Until this point, she had only been stung on her arms and legs. She didn't want to think about what might happen if a ghost's fingers ever passed through her heart.

Worried about just that possibility, Cordelia covered her chest as she leaped away from the trick-or-treater. She wasn't quite fast enough. The dead girl's fingers passed through her wrist, leaving behind a cold patch of skin. It was like being bitten by an ice spider. Cordelia ignored the pain and continued to stumble backward, windmilling her arms in order to maintain some semblance of balance. If she could only reach the end of the girl's ghost zone—the invisible barrier that tethered each spirit to a specific area of the school—Cordelia knew she would be safe.

"Behind you!" Benji exclaimed.

Cordelia grunted, more in surprise than pain, as her backside collided with something solid. At first she thought it was the wall of the attic. Then she heard a loud crash and realized that she had knocked one of Elijah Shadow's architectural models off its pedestal.

Great, Cordelia thought. *If this ghost doesn't kill me, Dr. Roqueni will.*

The trick-or-treater stopped less than a foot from Cordelia and pounded her tiny fists against invisible walls. The witch mask hung askew on her face, revealing a pale white chin and bloodless lips.

"I'm so sorry," Cordelia said, too ashamed to meet the girl's eyes. "This is our fault."

Benji scooped up the pile of miniature chocolates and approached the ghost. Cordelia waved him away, worried that the girl would redirect her anger now that Cordelia was beyond her reach, but Benji ignored her.

The girl turned to face him.

"I'm sorry too," he said, and dropped all the chocolates into the trick-or-treater's plastic pumpkin. Her Bright appeared instantly, a crisp autumn evening buzzing with laughter and doorbells.

The girl graced Benji and Cordelia with a smile of forgiveness and left the world of the living forever.

"How bad did she get you?" Benji asked, gently lifting her wrist. Cordelia met his deep brown eyes, soft with concern, and decided that she was no longer annoyed with him.

"Not as bad as I deserve," she said. "I'll be fine." She looked down at the house that she had knocked from its pedestal. "Maybe."

She knelt next to the model and ran her hand over its surface, checking for damage. It was a quaint cottage divided into two distinct styles: brick on the bottom half, green stucco with decorative wooden beams on top. A dozen black horseshoes climbed the chimney.

"I thought these models were all based on haunted houses," Benji said. "This one looks like something out of a fairy tale."

"Archimancy can work with any house, not just creepy old mansions," Cordelia said. "This is a Tudor Revival. That style was really popular around the time Mr. Shadow was doing his research."

Benji regarded her with surprise. "And you know this . . . how?"

"I've been watching a lot of YouTube videos. I figured it might be useful to learn more about architecture. Maybe we can understand how the school works."

"I already know how it works," Benji said. "Ghosts come. We make them go away." He slipped his hands beneath the model. "Help me put this back."

Working together, the two of them lifted the miniature house into place. Cordelia circled the pedestal to give it a final look and gasped in dismay when she saw the back roof. A section about the size of her hand had caved inward where it struck the floor.

"Oops," Benji said, gritting his teeth. "It's not so bad. Maybe Dr. Roqueni won't notice."

"Dr. Roqueni notices everything. We have to tell her."

"Not if we fix it," Benji suggested. He stuck his fingers into the hole, trying to tweeze the broken piece out. "How hard can it be? A little glue and it'll be good as—"

Another section of the roof crumbled beneath his hand, doubling the size of the hole.

"You're making it worse!" Cordelia exclaimed, yanking his hand away.

"I was trying to help!"

"I know," Cordelia said, peeking through the hole. The tiny bedroom below her was fully furnished with a four-poster bed, antique armoire, and standing mirror. Cordelia caught a whiff of something sweet and smoky, like a scented candle.

"Check out the details," she said. "There's furniture and everything. Even a tiny little book on the bedside table."

"But these models don't open up or anything," Benji said. "Why go through all that effort?"

"Elijah was trying to figure out what made these particular houses haunted. I guess that meant duplicating every detail on the inside as well, just in case there was something that—"

Hinges squeaked behind her. Cordelia spun around and saw a tall man in his late sixties step through the door connecting Dr. Roqueni's apartment and the attic. He was wearing a pair of glasses with black-tinted, triangular lenses. A small meter in his left hand, connected to the glasses by a thin black wire, clicked like a Geiger counter as he waved it back and forth.

The moment he saw Cordelia and Benji, the man grinned with childlike enthusiasm.

"Why, hello there!" he exclaimed. "How long have you two been dead?"

Shadows in the Attic

Cordelia and Benji stared at the strange man. The strange man stared back.

"We're not dead," Benji finally said.

"You can talk!" the man exclaimed, his smile wider than ever. "I had hoped these glasses would help me see the ghosts, but I never dreamed they'd help me hear them as well! This is spectacular!" He began to do a little jig, his boots tapping against the wooden floor. "Just wait until I tell the rest of my family. They said it was impossible, that only those born with the Sight were special enough to—"

"We're not ghosts," Benji said.

The man stopped dancing. "What do you mean?" he asked.

"We're just kids," Benji said. "*Living* kids."

"Of course you think that," the man replied with a sympathetic tone. "No one wants to believe that their time on earth has ended. But this is a very special building, and although you might not remember what happened, let me assure you that there's only one reason two children would be up here in the attic. You're ghosts."

Benji started to say something, but Cordelia stopped him. She had a theory about who this man might be, and she wanted to test it out. "Is that an EMF meter?" she asked, pointing toward the small machine in his hand. It was orange with a digital display.

The man nodded with a surprised expression. "How did you know that?" he asked.

Cordelia relaxed, her suspicion confirmed. Shadow School had developed a spooky reputation over the years, and every so often a former student mentioned it on a message board about haunted places. This man was clearly an amateur ghost hunter who had snuck in and decided to do some exploring.

"I know people use EMF meters to hunt ghosts," Cordelia said. "They believe spirits are nothing more than electromagnetic waves." Agnes had completely debunked this theory the previous year, but Cordelia decided not to add that part.

"*My* meter does a lot more than just tell you there's a ghost in the vicinity," the man said in a huff. He tapped his glasses with clear pride. "It gathers the electromagnetic radiation naturally present in any haunted house and uses it to power these lenses. That's what lets me see the ghosts. To be honest, before I saw you two, I was starting to wonder if they actually worked."

"So if you take the glasses off, we should disappear, right?" Cordelia asked.

"Naturally."

"Mind giving it a try?" Benji asked, catching on. "If I am a ghost, I'd like to know for sure."

"If it'll make you feel better," the man said.

He removed the glasses. Cordelia saw the light die in his eyes as he realized he could still see the two kids in front of him. "Well," he said, turning the glasses in his hands. "That's disappointing. I really thought I had it this time."

"Sorry," Cordelia said.

"If you're not dead," the man said, eyes narrowing, "then you're trespassing on private property." He looked past them, checking the rest of the attic. "I heard a loud crash up here. What were you two doing?"

"We're not trespassing," Benji said, ignoring his

question. "We go to school here. You're the one who shouldn't be here."

The man laughed. "My family owns this entire building," he said. "You have a school only because we've given this town permission to use our property." He stood tall and patted his chest. "I'm Darius Shadow."

Cordelia tried to keep her face impassive, as though she had never heard his name before, but fireworks were exploding in her head. Darius Shadow was Dr. Roqueni's uncle, and according to the principal, he was not a good man. She had warned them that he would come to visit at some point, and when he did, they had to conceal their abilities from him at all costs.

Although Darius was nowhere near as sinister as Cordelia had imagined, she trusted the principal's judgment.

Don't let him know we can see the ghosts, she thought.

"It's nice to meet you, Mr. Shadow," Cordelia said. "I'm sure you have a lot to do, so we'll get out of your way now . . ."

She started toward the door, but Darius blocked her path.

"You haven't answered my question," he said. "What are you two doing up here?"

"I already told you," Benji said. "We're students."

"It's summer. School's closed."

"We volunteered to help. There're boxes of school supplies that need to be delivered to the classrooms."

"That's the custodians' job."

"Usually," Cordelia said, aiming to seal the cracks in Benji's lie with a little truth. "Only Mr. Ward, the head custodian, retired a few weeks ago. We're just lending a hand until Dr. Roqueni hires a new guy."

Darius studied them with suspicious eyes. "Not bad," he said, as though he knew they were lying but appreciated the effort. "There are two flaws in your story, though. I don't see any boxes. And this isn't a classroom."

"We finished early today," Cordelia said. "So we decided to explore a little."

"And you just happened to end up here?" Darius asked, looking more dubious than ever. Cordelia understood why. There were only two ways to reach the attic: through Dr. Roqueni's apartment or the hidden passage behind the walls. A regular student wouldn't know about either one.

"We found this secret passageway!" Cordelia exclaimed, deciding that this was the more likely scenario. "It was soooo cool! But I guess you know all about that, Mr. Shadow, this being your family's building and all." She gazed around the attic, desperate to change the subject. "Are these dollhouses yours, too?"

"They're not *dollhouses*!" Darius exclaimed. He lovingly opened and closed the tiny iron gate of a Gothic mansion. "These are the most detailed architectural models the world has ever known. They should be in a museum. And they will be, one day, when the world finally understands the genius of Elijah Shadow."

Darius strode between the pedestals, pausing here and there to wipe away a smudge from a windowpane or straighten a tiny mailbox. Cordelia and Benji tracked his progress, moving as one to block his view of the broken model behind them.

"Each of these models was once a real place, you know," Darius said, "though most of them have succumbed to the ravages of time by now—or been burnt to the ground by their owners. Their stories live on, though. Grandma Wilma used to kneel by my bedside and tell me the strange and wonderful things that happened there. Ghost stories. Far too frightening for most children, especially these days, but I was captivated. My grandma Wilma could see them, you know. Ghosts." He looked down at the glasses in his hands and shoved them in his pocket. "Unfortunately, I didn't inherit her gift."

Darius considered the two children before him and scratched his bald pate. "Here I am," he said, "a strange old man talking about ghost stories. And neither one of you seems the slightest bit surprised. And what kind of girl can identify an EMF meter?" Darius lifted an old brass key that hung from a leather cord around his neck and rubbed it between his fingers. "It makes me wonder. Perhaps you have a certain degree of experience in this area. Hmm? Maybe you didn't just find a secret passageway. Maybe you know a lot more about Shadow School than you really should." He leaned over the roof of a dilapidated bungalow and searched their eyes. "Tell me, my new friends. Have you ever seen a ghost?"

Before Cordelia could fashion an appropriate reply, Dr. Roqueni burst through the door. The principal usually put a lot of care into her stylish appearance (inspiring the snarky moniker "Dr. Vogue" in the PTO Facebook group), but she looked uncharacteristically disheveled: shirt untucked, glasses askew.

Cordelia had never been happier to see her.

"There you are," Dr. Roqueni said, catching her breath. "I've been looking everywhere for you."

For a moment, Cordelia wasn't sure if she was talking about the children or her uncle. Then she saw the pleading look in Dr. Roqueni's eyes—*Play along!*—and realized that the next line in their improvised script belonged to her.

"Sorry, Dr. Roqueni," Cordelia replied. "I know we

were supposed to be working, but we found a secret passageway on the third floor! Come on—we'll show you!"

"Oh, *that*," Dr. Roqueni said, as though secret passageways were as common as kitchen sinks. "Just a fluke of an old house. Nothing more to it."

Darius fixed her with an incredulous gaze. "These children claim they were helping you—"

"Deliver school supplies to the classrooms," Dr. Roqueni said without missing a beat. They had prepared this story beforehand, just in case an adult ever questioned the children's presence in the school. "That's correct. Though they weren't supposed to be helping me *today*. In fact, I had no idea they were even in the school until I happened to see their bikes outside. If they had bothered to ask, I would have informed them that I had a surprise visitor and they should *stay home*."

Cordelia felt her face grow warm. They were only supposed to come to the school on pre-arranged days. This wasn't one of them.

"Sorry," Cordelia said. "I guess we just really wanted to . . . deliver as many boxes as possible."

"Speak for yourself," Benji muttered. "I was happy playing FIFA."

"I appreciate your work ethic," Dr. Roqueni said. "But perhaps this is a sign that you need a little break. Take the rest of the summer off. You deserve it."

Cordelia's mouth fell open. "But there are so many more . . . boxes to deliver!" she exclaimed. "And more boxes arrive every day, so if we fall behind, they're just going to pile up and we'll never–"

"This isn't up for debate, Cordelia," Dr. Roqueni said with a warning tone in her voice. "I've been thinking about this for some time now, and I've come to the decision that it's unhealthy for any child to spend so much time in school." She placed her hands on Cordelia's shoulders. "It's summer, for goodness' sake! Go swimming. Eat ice cream. Have *fun*."

"Works for me," Benji said, tugging Cordelia in the direction of the trapdoor. "We won't tell anyone else about the secret passageway, Dr. R. Mum's the word. See you in September!"

Cordelia shot him a look of betrayal. *How can he just give up like that? The ghosts need us!* She wished she could plead her case to Dr. Roqueni, but Darius already seemed suspicious enough. She didn't want to make things worse.

"Fine," Cordelia said. She turned to Darius. "It was nice to meet you, Mr. Shadow." To her surprise, she actually meant it. Despite Dr. Roqueni's warnings, she had found the strange old man endearing–and it was clear that he loved the ghosts as much as she did.

"It was nice to meet you too," said Darius.

"Bye, Cordelia," Dr. Roqueni said. "Enjoy your break."

Cordelia followed Benji down the ladder, already feeling depressed. *Two months? With no ghosts at all? What was she going to do?*

Her summer was ruined.

4

Ezra

For the rest of the summer, the sprits of Shadow School haunted the corridors of Cordelia's mind. *Do they think I've abandoned them?* she wondered, lying awake at night as their old air conditioner rattled like the chains of a Dickensian ghost. *Are they lonely? Are they mad?* These concerns plunged Cordelia into moods dark enough to eclipse the August sun. She spent entire days holed up in her bedroom, researching spectral phenomena so she could be as prepared as possible when she finally continued her duties. Agnes visited her father in Boston. Benji babysat his sisters while their parents were at work. The three friends texted one another often, but every time Agnes and Cordelia started talking about something productive, Benji steered the conversation to boring kid stuff: movies, sports, the latest gossip. Anything other than ghosts.

He didn't understand.

It was only after visiting her grandparents in San Francisco that Cordelia realized the entire summer was about to slip through her fingertips. She dedicated herself to a strong finish, making memories at a feverish clip: sharing a blanket with her parents while watching fireworks in the park, bike riding with Agnes and discovering a covered bridge, brushing her fingers against Benji's as they rode the Ferris wheel at the Ludlow Carnival.

Even then, the ghosts were never far from her thoughts. When Cordelia exited the bus that first day of school, the relief nearly made her knees buckle.

I can finally help them again, she thought. *I can finally do what I was meant to do.*

Cordelia spotted Agnes struggling to make her way through the crowd while dragging a rolling backpack behind her. She was taller than most of the other students, with long, blond hair corralled into an efficient braid.

Cordelia greeted her with a huge hug.

"Happy first day of school!" Agnes exclaimed, flashing her violet braces in a smile. She handed Cordelia a brown paper bag. "I made you a brownie to celebrate.

Dark chocolate and toasted marshmallow. I'm not sure if it's any good."

"You always say that, and it's always perfect."

"And here's your schedule," Agnes said, handing Cordelia a plastic folder. "I printed you a copy because I knew you'd forget."

"Or maybe I forgot because I knew you'd print me a copy. Who's the smart one now?"

"Still me. I'm psyched that Dr. Roqueni put us all in the same homeroom. Fighting evil spirits with the principal has its benefits."

"Where is Dr. Roqueni, anyway?" Cordelia asked, scanning the parking lot. "She's usually out here directing traffic."

"I'm sure she's around. Are you still mad at her for kicking you out?"

"I'm over it. Not looking forward to telling her about the model I broke, though. Do you think she's noticed by now?"

"Probably," Agnes said. "Better to just tell her and get it over with."

Cordelia ate her brownie and observed the other students pouring through the front gate. Most of them were wearing outfits so new you could practically hear the tags being snipped off. Cordelia suddenly felt self-conscious about her own clothes: sneakers, jogging shorts, and a simple T-shirt. She had been so focused on dressing for comfort—knowing that she would be running around and helping ghosts after school—that she had forgotten all about style.

Cordelia caught sight of Benji heading in their direction. A pretty girl with a mass of curly dark hair was walking next to him. He waved goodbye, and she gave him a huge smile before joining a group of passing girls.

"Who was that?" Cordelia asked Benji, trying to sound as casual as possible.

"Viviana Martínez. She's cool."

"But not as cool as me," Agnes said, handing him a brownie and a copy of his schedule. "We have Mrs. Machen for math again, but all our other teachers are new."

"Ugh. Machen," Benji said.

"She's not so bad," Agnes said. "She gave me a trigonometry textbook to read over the summer. It was fun!"

"Fun?" Benji asked.

"You play with a ball. I play with numbers."

Cordelia leaned closer to Agnes. "Did you bring your goggles?"

Agnes looked surprised by the question. "Okay, first of all, we're calling them spectercles now," she said. "Spectacles. Specters. Get it?"

"Cute," Cordelia said.

"Yeah, but I left them at home. I know they're invisible, so it's not like anyone would even know I'm wearing them, but it's the first day of school. I didn't think we were—"

"No worries," Cordelia said. "You can use one of the extra pairs."

"You seriously want to rescue ghosts today?" Benji asked. "Can't we just take a few days to ease into it?"

"You've had the entire summer off, Benji," Cordelia said. "Those poor ghosts have been trapped for months. They shouldn't have to wait another day!"

Benji looked like he wanted to argue, then gave a sigh of acceptance. "All right, boss," he said. "Back to work."

"I'm in too," Agnes said. "As long as our teachers don't give us much home—"

"Shh," Benji said. "It's too early for the H-word. I can't take it."

They passed through the gate and beneath a sheltering canopy of maples and elms. The school towered over them, unfurling its massive shadow like a cloak. Cordelia could already see several new ghosts in the windows, including a girl waving a red-and-black flag and a man wearing an astronaut helmet.

Cordelia's heart fluttered with anticipation. She couldn't wait to get started.

"Give it back!" someone exclaimed.

A small crowd had gathered outside the doors of the school to watch three seventh graders tease a gangly fifth-grade boy. Cordelia was completely unsurprised to see Mason James at the head of the pack. He had gotten taller over the summer and his shoulders had filled out. The cruel twist of his smile hadn't changed at all.

"I'm doing you a favor," Mason said. He was holding a stuffed wolf over his head, far too high for the leaping fifth grader to reach. "What are you, ten? Eleven? You bring this to school, you're gonna get teased. Kids can be mean, you know?"

Mason laughed, impressed by his own cleverness. The two other boys laughed as well. The fifth grader looked close to tears.

"Looks like your bullying techniques didn't get rusty over the summer," Agnes said.

"Thanks, Geekzilla," Mason said, taking her words as a genuine compliment. He looked over their group and seemed to forget about his prey for the moment. "Check it out, boys. It's the freak patrol. You three gonna spend the entire year sneaking around the school and whispering in corners again?"

"Just leave the kid alone, Mason," Benji said. "It's his first day here."

Mason considered the request. Benji was afforded a

certain degree of respect due to his skill on the soccer field. At one point, he and Mason had even been friends.

"Why are you still hanging with these weirdos, Núñez? You used to be cool."

"I'm still cool," Benji said with a grin. "And I don't need to pick on fifth graders to prove it."

The morning bell rang.

"Enough of you losers," Mason said, tossing the stuffed wolf to the ground. He and his minions made sure to step on it on their way inside the school.

Cordelia brushed the dirt off the wolf and handed it to the boy.

"Thanks," he said, slipping the stuffed animal inside his backpack before it could cause any more trouble. He was an odd-looking kid. It seemed like the various parts of his body were growing at different rates, leaving him with a large nose and long legs, but short arms and tiny eyes. His face was covered with freckles.

"What's your name?" Cordelia asked.

"Ezra," he said, surprising Cordelia by shaking her hand. "Ezra Gottfried. This is all my fault. I should have gone straight inside just like Mom said. But look at this place! What kind of school is this?" He gestured at the building with bulging, terrified eyes. "I took Drool out of my backpack just to feel a little braver until I got inside. I know I'm too old for stuffed animals. I don't, like, sleep with him or anything."

Cordelia could tell from Ezra's blushing face that he definitely slept with Drool, probably every single night. But she nodded as though she believed him.

"I was scared my first day too," Cordelia said. "Here's the thing: Shadow School may look scary, but there's nothing here that can hurt you. I mean, it's still school, so don't expect Disney World or anything. But I promise you'll be okay."

That got a hint of a smile. They started to walk toward the entrance together.

"Who's your homeroom teacher?" Benji asked.

"Mrs. King."

"I had her!" Agnes exclaimed. "She's super nice. She lets you play board games every Friday afternoon and has a pet gecko named Lemonade."

"I had a pet gecko once," Ezra said. "My mom vacuumed it up by accident. At least, I think it was by accident. Mom doesn't like animals." He stopped before the threshold of the school. "Are you sure it isn't haunted?"

"Don't be silly, Ezra," said Cordelia, guiding him around an old fisherman standing in the doorway and looking longingly at the beautiful day outside. "There's no such thing as ghosts."

The fisherman's pole was missing its line. Cordelia made a mental note of it for later.

5

Mr. Derleth's Discovery

In all her time at Shadow School, Cordelia had never seen so many ghosts. They were everywhere: sitting on desks, crouched beneath tables, peeking out from behind vent covers. While her new teachers droned on about rules and procedures, Cordelia formulated a mental list of the Brightkeys she would need after school. *Jump rope for the girl in the gym. Chalk for the man staring at the blackboard. Shoelaces and earbuds for all the new joggers.*

At last, the final bell rang. Cordelia, Agnes, and Benji lingered by their lockers until the mob of students thinned out, then descended a spiral staircase to the basement. A locked door with an intimidating sign blocked their path:

NO STUDENTS OR TEACHERS BEYOND THIS POINT
HAZARDOUS AIR QUALITY

Dr. Roqueni had given each of them a key to the door. Agnes used hers, and the trio stepped into a long, dark hallway. It was eerily silent. Over the summer, teachers who taught in the basement had been reassigned to higher floors due to "emergency asbestos removal." It wasn't a permanent solution, but for now the kids could enter and leave Elijah Shadow's office without the risk of being seen.

"I can't believe Dr. Roqueni let the ghosts pile up like this," Cordelia said, sidestepping a pigtailed girl holding a ceramic unicorn. "She should have let us stay and do our thing."

"With her uncle still here?" Benji asked. "No way. He was already suspicious enough. If we kept showing up at the school, he definitely would have figured out we can see the ghosts."

"So what?" Agnes asked, sliding her spectercles on. She leaned against Cordelia's shoulder a moment, allowing the dizziness to pass as her eyes adjusted to seeing two worlds at once. "Why is Dr. Roqueni so afraid of her uncle finding out that you have the Sight?"

Cordelia hesitated before answering. Dr. Roqueni had told her the story several months ago, but she wasn't sure whether it had been in confidence.

They're your best friends, Cordelia thought. *They deserve to know.*

"He was a jerk to her when she was our age," Cordelia said. "She doesn't want him to do the same thing to us."

"What did he do?" Benji asked.

"Mr. Shadow can't see the ghosts, right? And it's a thing with him. So he used little Dr. Roqueni to see them instead." Cordelia could tell from their baffled expressions that she wasn't explaining it the right way, so she tried a different approach. "You know Katie? How her mom really wanted to be an actress but all she ever really did was that one commercial with the singing vacuum cleaner, so now she makes Katie take all those acting classes even though she doesn't actually want to?"

"Katie Tran takes acting classes?" Agnes asked.

"Not Katie Tran," Cordelia said. "Katie Waters."

"Katie Tran plays the guitar," Benji said.

Agnes shook her head. "You're thinking of Katie Millhauser. With the hats."

"Too many Katies," Benji said.

"Anyway," Cordelia continued, "Mr. Shadow forced Dr. Roqueni to roam around Shadow School and tell him about all the ghosts so he could know what they were like. He took her to a bunch of other supposedly haunted houses, too, just to see if her gift would work there. This went on for years. Dr. Roqueni said he used to call her his 'Little Eyes.'"

"Why didn't her parents tell this guy to go away?" Benji asked.

"Bad mom," Cordelia said. "Dead dad."

"Well, Dr. Roqueni has nothing to worry about with us," Benji said. "We're not Shadows. Our parents aren't going to let us go off on ghost-hunting adventures with a crazy old man."

"He's not crazy," Cordelia said. "I actually feel kind of bad for him. He was so disappointed when he found out his special ghost-seeing glasses didn't work!"

Agnes gave her a strange look. "You sound like you like him," she said.

Cordelia shrugged.

"The way Dr. Roqueni described him, I thought he was going to be really mean and scary. But he's just this grandpa who's proud that he's related to Elijah Shadow and wishes that he could see ghosts like the rest of his family. Maybe he's not as bad as Dr. Roqueni said."

"Or maybe we don't know the whole story," Benji said.

They stopped in front of a bulletin board covered with yellowed artwork from the previous year. After a quick check of the hallway in either direction, Cordelia pressed a special hibiscus concealed in the flowered wallpaper while Agnes pressed its twin. The floor opened, revealing a set of stairs that led into the darkness.

"Our school rules," Agnes said with a grin.

They descended the stairs and used a lever to close the floor above them. Elijah Shadow's office had been a dark, rat-infested mess when they discovered it last year. Its renovation was still a work in progress, but significant improvements had been made. Before retiring and moving to Greece, Mr. Ward—the former head custodian of Shadow School and one of the few adults who knew about the ghosts—had rewired the outdated electrical connections and installed modern light fixtures. The floors had been swept and mopped, walls scrubbed, books shelved. They had even reorganized the adjoining storage room with a variety of possible Brightkeys.

Mr. Derleth, who had learned about the ghosts when Cordelia helped his son last year, was sitting at the drafting table in the center of the room, flipping through one of Elijah's journals while making notes on a yellow legal pad. A nasty bruise darkened his left cheekbone.

"Whoa!" Benji exclaimed. "What happened, Mr.

D? You get into a fight?"

"In a manner of speaking," Mr. Derleth said. "Dr. Roqueni and I attempted to move Elijah's bones so we could inter him properly in the Shadow family crypt. He took exception. The last thing I remember before blacking out is a particularly thick volume of architectural history flying toward my face."

Cordelia glanced over at the cot where Elijah Shadow had taken his final breath. Now that the office had been refurbished, his skeleton looked as out of place as a snowman on a beach. Elijah's ghost stood over his remains. His white shirt was forever rolled up at the sleeves, his mustache neat and trim.

"That wasn't very nice," Cordelia scolded him. "Mr. Derleth was just trying to help."

Elijah crossed his arms, daring anyone else to touch his bones.

"He feels really awful that you got hurt," Cordelia told Mr. Derleth.

"Yeah, right," Mr. Derleth replied with a dubious look. He couldn't see the ghosts, though one time he had tried out Agnes's spectercles to experience what it was like. After a short walk through the school, Mr. Derleth had returned—face ashen, hands shaking—and announced that he was better suited for research.

"How's it going?" Cordelia asked, picking up one

of Elijah's journals from a nearby stack and flipping through its pages. Tiny handwriting covered every millimeter of white space, broken only by the occasional sketch or diagram.

"Slow and steady," Mr. Derleth replied. "My goal was to finish all of Elijah's journals by the end of the summer, but it's going to take a lot longer than that. Elijah suffered from an obsessive need to write down every single thought that came into his head. Some of them are brilliant. Others not so much. His poem about toenails was a particular low point."

Cordelia smiled. Mr. Derleth had always seemed sad last year—with good reason—but lately he had begun to joke around a little bit. She hoped this was a sign of things to come.

"Welcome back, children," Dr. Roqueni said, entering the office. "Sorry I haven't had a chance to say hello. I've been stuck in my office, planning the agendas for our upcoming faculty meetings."

Dr. Roqueni didn't offer a smile or ask them how their summers had been. *Is she mad at me?* Cordelia wondered, an uneasy feeling gnawing at her stomach. *Does she know I broke the horseshoe house?*

"*More* faculty meetings?" Mr. Derleth asked. "If I had known that's why you wanted to clean out the conservatory, I never would have agreed to help."

"I think it looks lovely," Dr. Roqueni said. "There are even more plants being delivered next week. Now that the ghost snatchers are no longer an issue, I can finally focus on the *school* part of Shadow School. Especially if . . ." She paused and shared a long look with Mr. Derleth. "Have you told them yet?"

"No—I was waiting for you."

"Told us what?" Cordelia asked.

Mr. Derleth took a moment to stand up and stretch, then leaned against the drafting table and faced the children. "Two years before he faked his own death, Elijah concluded that Shadow School—or Shadow Manor, as it was known back then—had been a terrible mistake. He hadn't always felt that way. In his younger years, Elijah had cast himself in the role of rescuer, the ghosts as refugees from a bleak and barren world. It was only years later, when he saw the first ghost accept its 'final gift' and ascend into its 'hereafter'—what we call Brightkeys and Brights—that Elijah began to question his earlier assessment. There was no denying the joy in the ghosts' faces as they escaped the school."

"Elijah finally accepted the fact that he wasn't a rescuer," Dr. Roqueni said with surprising ire. "He was a captor."

Cordelia glanced in Elijah's direction. The ghost bowed his head in shame.

"Elijah became obsessed with undoing the damage he had done," Mr. Derleth said. "That's why he set that fire in the attic and faked his own death. Any party interested in using his research for their own endeavors would believe it had all been destroyed. And being 'dead' allowed him to work undisturbed."

"The school is only haunted because of the way it's built," Benji said, hopping up on one of the long cabinets that housed Elijah's vast collection of blueprints. "So why not knock down a wall or two and mess with the archimancy?"

"We've been over this before," Cordelia said. "That's not the way it works."

"Shouldn't we at least *try* it? If someone gives me a sledgehammer, I'd be happy to do a little experiment—"

"Don't you *dare*!" Dr. Roqueni exclaimed, startling all of them. Benji's face turned pale. Even at her sternest, the principal wasn't one to raise her voice.

"I was just joking," Benji muttered.

"Sorry," Dr. Roqueni said, grimacing. "I didn't mean to shout. But you need to understand that if you break the bonds of archimancy that hold this place together, there will be a release of spectral energy powerful enough to destroy all the spirits in the school. They'll stop existing altogether. No afterlife. No Bright. 'Knock down a wall or two,' and you condemn the ghosts to a

45

fate far worse than death."

Dr. Roqueni massaged her temples, wincing as though she had a headache. There were dark circles under her eyes. *Guess the visit from her uncle didn't go so great,* Cordelia thought.

"But there was a fire in the attic," Agnes said. "That must have done enough damage to impact the archimancy."

"Usually that would be the case," Mr. Derleth said. "But Elijah knew what was at risk and made sure the fire was contained to a 'nonessential' area of the house. After that, he hid in this office and tried to figure out a way to send the ghosts safely on their way. It wasn't easy. Archimancy was"–he consulted his notes—"'a stubborn cage that refused to relinquish the poor souls trapped behind its bars.' After years of work, however, Elijah finally succeeded in designing a machine capable of dehaunting the school completely."

Benji hopped down from the file cabinet. "Hold on," he said. "Are you saying what I think you're saying? Elijah invented a machine that can make all the ghosts go away?"

Mr. Derleth nodded. "Want to see it?" he asked with a smile.

6

The Dehaunter

Dr. Roqueni led them to an oil painting of a crowded park. The men wore suits and hats, and the women carried parasols to shield themselves from the summer sun. Children played on the edge of a lake.

"One of Elijah's more playful secrets," Dr. Roqueni said. "In order to open the door, you need to find the ghost hidden in the park."

"Fun!" Cordelia said, studying the painting. At first she checked the figures for obvious signs, such as transparency or a missing shadow. When that didn't lead anywhere, she searched for other details. One man had dirt beneath his fingernails. A girl was having trouble opening her parasol. A dog barked at a frightened child.

"It's the woman in the white dress," Cordelia said. "By the tree."

Dr. Roqueni looked surprised by how quickly Cordelia had figured out the answer. "How did you know?" the principal asked.

"Everyone else is doing something. Either talking or playing or looking at the pretty view. But the woman is just watching them. That's all she can do. She wants to be part of the fun, too. But she can't because she's dead." Cordelia stepped closer and saw the desperate longing in the woman's eyes, confirming her theory. "It looks like a happy painting, but it's actually sad."

"I agree," Dr. Roqueni said.

Remembering the hibiscuses that opened the trapdoor to Elijah's office, Cordelia pressed on the ghost in the painting and felt a hidden button move. The entire painting clicked open like a door. Behind it, a ladder descended into a dark chute. Dr. Roqueni led the way, and the rest of them followed. By the time Cordelia's feet finally touched the floor, she suspected they were lower than the basement. The air was cold and musty.

Cordelia examined this new room.

Unlike the rest of Shadow School, which was decorated in the ornate fashion of a classic Victorian home, the space here was spartan and bare. Dirt floors. Brick walls. A workbench with lots of drawers.

And a house in the center of the room.

It was much larger than the models in the attic but just as precisely detailed, a hodgepodge of styles that had been patched together into something strange and wonderful. Cordelia peeked through one of the windows and saw that unlike its smaller cousins, the inside of this house was not furnished at all. Instead, copper wire ran along the walls and ceilings of its twisting corridors, like the inner workings of a complex machine.

"I'd be lying if I claimed to understand exactly how this thing works," Mr. Derleth said. "But here's what I've managed to piece together from Elijah's journals. Raw spectral energy is gathered from all the ghosts in the school and sent down here through those copper wires coming from the ceiling. That energy passes through the house and—through the power of archimancy—transforms into something Elijah called activation mist." Mr. Derleth pointed to two sets of pipes—one purple, one green—that protruded from the roof of the house and branched off into dozens of holes in the ceiling. "These pipes take the mist up to the mirrors on the fourth floor, which then allow the spirits safe passage out of Shadow School. He called it a dehaunter."

"Sick," Benji said.

"What exactly does 'safe passage' mean?" Cordelia asked. "Do the mirrors turn into Brights?"

"That was Elijah's goal," Dr. Roqueni said. "But he worried that this was a feat even archimancy couldn't accomplish. He thought the ghosts might have to settle for passage beyond the walls of the school, where they could find someplace better to haunt–perhaps the place they were *meant* to haunt, before Shadow School stole them away." Her brows furrowed. "Near the end, Elijah stopped writing in his journals, so I can't tell you what his final decision was."

"As long as the ghosts are gone, who cares?" Benji asked, looking around the room. "How do we turn this thing on?"

"Settle down, Mr. Núñez. It isn't that easy. Check the back of the house."

Holding herself for warmth, Cordelia circled the dehaunter and immediately saw the problem. The house wasn't finished. At least two rooms in the top floor were missing, along with part of the roof.

"Elijah died before he could complete it," Dr. Roqueni said.

"I guess this isn't one of those close-enough kind of deals?" Benji asked as Agnes wandered over to the workbench.

"You know how it is with archimancy," Dr. Roqueni said. "Everything has to be perfect, or it won't work at all. And unfortunately, we don't know what those last few rooms should look like. Elijah was rushing at the end. I presume he knew his days were numbered, so he was working without a blueprint."

"He left notes, though," Agnes said, flipping through a pile of yellowed sheets. Cordelia peeked over her shoulder and saw a riot of diagrams and equations that made her head spin. "Formulas. Equations. Maybe we could use these."

"Unfortunately, Dr. Roqueni and I can't make heads or tails of them," Mr. Derleth said. "The math is just beyond us."

"It's not too bad," Agnes said, totally absorbed in what she was reading. "Mostly trig and linear algebra. And what I think might be geometric topology. I watched a few college lectures on YouTube, but a lot of it went over my head. I'd have to really sit down and study it . . . his equations are *beautiful*!"

Cordelia saw Mr. Derleth give Dr. Roqueni a smile. "Told you she could do it," he said.

"We'll see," said Dr. Roqueni.

"See what?" Agnes asked.

"If you're capable of finishing the plans for the dehaunter," said Dr. Roqueni.

Agnes looked at her as if she had gone completely insane. "I can't do that!" Agnes exclaimed, tugging at her braid. "That's a big deal! That's . . . you need an engineer or a mathematician or an architect."

"What we need is a genius," Mr. Derleth said. "And we have one. Right here."

"I'm not a genius," Agnes said. "I just understand things that nobody else does."

"That's literally what a genius is," Cordelia whispered.

"But what if I mess up?" Agnes asked.

"Then you mess up," Benji said. "No big deal. Just think of it like a test."

"Yes," said Dr. Roqueni. "That's perfect. A test."

Agnes looked down at the pages in her hands. "I like tests," she muttered. "Tests are fun. . . ." She smiled stiffly. "I guess I could give it a try."

Benji whooped with joy and ran around the room high-fiving everyone. Cordelia played along, but she wasn't sure how she felt. If they dehaunted the school, they could save a lot of ghosts. That was a good thing. But it also meant her days of helping the ghosts would be over, and the thought saddened her. Who would she be without them?

It was four thirty by the time they got back to the office. Cordelia tried to talk Agnes and Benji into staying for just a little while longer, but they were tired and their parents were already on their way, so they headed outside. Cordelia knew she should probably join them. After all, her father was picking her up at five o'clock, and she had promised him she would be more punctual this year. But the desire to free the ghosts had been burning within her all day long, and Cordelia knew she wouldn't be able to sleep that night unless she doused its flame.

Just one, she thought, stocking up on Brightkeys. *Then straight home.*

She ran to a vacated art classroom where she had noticed a woman wearing a black wet suit and carrying a surfboard. The surfer had no interest in sunglasses or a towel, but a pair of earplugs finally did the trick. As the woman's spirit rose into her Bright, unleashing the sounds of seagulls and crashing waves, Cordelia felt a satisfying warmth fill her body. It was like returning home after being away for far too long.

This is what I was meant to do. This is who I am.

One ghost wasn't enough, however; there were so many others who needed her help! She ran down halls, up staircases, into classrooms, filling Brights with new residents. Time passed in a euphoric blur. When she finally remembered to check her phone, Cordelia was surprised to find several texts from her father, who was waiting outside and beginning to get worried.

Almost an hour had passed. It had felt like minutes.

Just one more, Cordelia thought, remembering the old gardener who hadn't wanted the trowel she offered him. *He's probably been waiting for me to return all summer long with the right Brightkey. It would be cruel to make him wait a single minute longer!*

After shooting her dad a quick text (Art club meeting running late. Five minutes! Sorry!), Cordelia ran upstairs, taking the steps two at a time. She reached a narrow hallway carpeted in red and gold. The walls were lined with oval-framed portraits of bearded men and high-collared ladies. The only sign that Cordelia was standing in a school and not a private home was an abandoned lunch bag.

The teachers' room was opposite an eighth-grade classroom that belonged to either Mrs. Link or Mrs. LaValle—Cordelia always got them confused. She opened the door and flicked on the light.

The gardener was standing on the large table in the center of the room.

His back was turned toward Cordelia, but there was no mistaking his large-brimmed sun hat and dirty gloves. Beneath his feet sat a nearly empty platter of baked goods. Cordelia imagined the teachers eating their cookies and scones, unaware of the ghost standing mere inches away from them. The thought wasn't as funny as it should have been.

"Good afternoon," Cordelia said. "Remember me? I didn't have what you needed last time, so I thought I'd try something new."

The gardener didn't turn around. Cordelia considered circling the table so she could meet the man's eyes, then decided against it. Ghosts were a finicky lot, and if the old man didn't want to look in her direction, it was best not to push it.

Cordelia slid her bookbag off her shoulders and placed it on the table as gently as possible. The silence was fragile.

"I've been thinking about why some Brightkeys work while others don't," Cordelia said. "And I think it's a question of need. See, a Bright is like heaven, only it isn't all angels and clouds, because that's not for everyone. A Bright takes you to whatever you loved most in life. The thing we do that never gets old! Skiing. The beach. Even jogging, for a lot of crazy people." Cordelia withdrew a small white packet from the side pocket of her bag. "I guess you liked to garden, huh? My *nainai* does too. Vegetables mostly. A trowel sure would be useful, but you don't exactly *need* it. Seeds, on the other hand? There's no way to garden without them."

Cordelia emptied the packet of tomato seeds onto the table. They barely made a sound, but the old man spun around as though a dozen cannons had fired. He gazed down at her with a snarl, and Cordelia stumbled backward, heart pounding. This clearly wasn't the nice sort of gardener who left baskets of fresh vegetables on his neighbor's stoop. This was the kind who sprinkled poison pellets for any rabbits or deer unlucky enough to trespass in his domain.

With a quick movement, he plucked a seed between two fingers.

A black triangle opened above the ghost, spreading rays of sunlight across the room. The smell of fresh mulch overpowered the odors of burnt popcorn and microwaved lunches.

The man began to rise.

Instead of welcoming his Bright, however, the gardener rebelled against it, tilting his body downward until he was rising feetfirst in the air, his hands desperately reaching out for some kind of purchase. It was as though the triangle was pulling him toward a black hole, not a warm spring afternoon. Finally, just as the gardener's feet had crossed the threshold between this world and the next, the ghost remembered the seed in his hand and tossed it away like a live grenade.

The triangle closed, and the ghost fell to the table.

He crouched down and slapped the rest of the seeds off the table. They hit Cordelia in the chest and pattered to the ground. The ghost reared back, readying himself to leap across the room and punish the girl who had tried to save him.

Cordelia didn't stop running until she reached her father's car.

The Missing Ghost

Cordelia met her friends by the lockers the next morning and ushered them through the slow-moving river of students. The school was still stretching its arms after a long night's slumber. Bleary-eyed teachers scrambled to put the finishing touches on lessons while fortifying themselves with coffee. Even the ghosts looked tired.

The children scaled the stairs two at a time and entered the teachers' room.

Ms. Straub, the health teacher, was staring out the window with a pensive expression. Someone had left an order form for Girl Scout Cookies on the big table.

The gardener was nowhere to be found.

"He was right here!" Cordelia exclaimed, checking beneath the table. "I don't understand!"

Ms. Straub turned her head and took in the three intruders. "You're not supposed to be here," she said.

"Sorry!" Benji exclaimed, dragging Cordelia out of the room. "She thought she left her water bottle here."

They headed toward the east stairwell, squeezing their way through the eighth graders who packed the narrow hallway. Cordelia was already one of the smallest kids in the seventh grade, but she felt like a toddler among the older kids.

"There was a ghost there yesterday," she said. "I'm not making it up."

"You don't need to convince us," Agnes said, slipping her spectercles into their case. "We're all believers here."

"I'll check the second floor," Benji said. "Ghost zones stretch in all directions. Maybe your gardener slipped through the floor of the teachers' room for a change of scenery."

"It's worth a look," Cordelia allowed, though she doubted they'd find anything useful. Even though ghosts had the ability to pass through walls and floors, they tended to avoid doing so unless they had a good reason.

"What did you do with those seeds you gave him?" Agnes asked.

"Left them on the floor," Cordelia said. "Why?"

"This is just a theory," Agnes said, yanking her rolling backpack over a buckle in the carpet, "but what if he changed his mind and picked up the seeds after you left? He might have entered his Bright then. That would explain why he isn't here anymore."

"No way," Cordelia said. "This guy *really* didn't want to go into his Bright. He wouldn't have changed his mind."

"Well, he's not going to have a choice next time," Benji said. "When Agnes gets that dehaunter running, he'll be kicked out whether he likes it or not."

"*If* Agnes gets the dehaunter running," Agnes said. "Which isn't a sure thing. There are still a lot of problems I need to solve."

"You'll figure it out," Benji said with a wave of his hand.

"That's easy for you to say," Agnes muttered. "You don't have to teach yourself fractal geometry."

Cordelia stopped them in the middle of the hallway. She was getting annoyed that her friends seemed to care more about dehaunting the school than what happened with the gardener.

"Do you understand how weird this is?" she asked. "I gave a ghost the key to his own personal paradise, and he was like, 'Nah. I'm just gonna spend eternity in this dark and dreary school instead.' That is *not* normal."

"Except he didn't stay here," Agnes whispered as students passed them on either side. "He's gone. I think he went to his Bright. That's the most logical explanation."

"I told you, there's no way that–"

"Why are you stressing about this, Cord?" Benji asked. "We should be focused on dehaunting the entire school, not a single ghost. We do that, and all our problems are solved. We'll never have to think about ghosts again. Isn't that what we all want?"

Agnes gave a hesitant nod. "I'll miss studying them," she said. "But it'll be nice to know they're all safe and sound."

Cordelia said nothing at all.

Most teachers quit working at Shadow School within a year or two. The ones who stuck around *liked* working in a creepy old Victorian mansion, which usually meant they were pretty strange.

Cordelia's new teachers were no exception.

Mr. Hearn, who taught social studies, was obsessed with natural disasters and left a new "fun fact" on the board every day ("The Shaanxi earthquake of 1556 killed over 800,000 people!" "Texas has more tornadoes per year than any other state!"). Ms. Gilman, their language arts teacher, kept a row of Venus flytraps on her desk and fed them the "flagrant misspellings" and "unnecessary adverbs" that she clipped from student essays.

From the moment she entered his classroom, Cordelia could tell that her art teacher, Mr. Keene, would be just as strange as the others.

He was sitting cross-legged on top of his desk, wearing a papier-mâché mask with two horns and large, bulbous eyes. Cordelia would have thought he was a ghost had the students in front of her not jumped in surprise. Clearly they could see him as well as she could.

"Good morning, Mr. Keene," Francesca said, barely looking up from the book she was reading as she passed. She had been in the Art Club the previous year so she already knew him. "Cool mask."

"Thanks," said Mr. Keene. "I made it this summer. Good book?"

"They're all good," she replied with a smile.

After claiming a paint-stained table with Benji and Agnes, Cordelia took a look around the classroom. Dozens of masks—the work, she suspected, of Mr. Keene's former students—hung from the walls: a horse with tufts of painted cotton for fur; a pig whose ear had fallen off, exposing a triangle of yellowed newspaper; a green monster with toothpick teeth; a baby with tiny Slinkys for eyes; and perhaps strangest of all, a simple white mask with question marks written all over it.

"As you may have noticed," Mr. Keene said, "I have a thing with masks. Always have, ever since I was a little kid. Don't worry, though. I also like hockey, barbecues, and classic rock. I'm not *that* weird."

Mr. Keene removed the mask from his face, revealing a middle-aged man with a pleasant, pudgy face. Cordelia could imagine him standing by a cart on a sunny afternoon and making balloon animals for children.

"You'll all get to make masks this year," he said, with a gap-toothed smile. "But this is only our first meeting, my friends, so no need to rush into things. For today, just relax and draw me anything you'd like. Let's see what you can do."

There was a tray of paper at the center of their table, as well as bins of markers and colored pencils. Cordelia took the third piece of paper from the top—the first two were a little crinkled—and removed a single 2B graphite pencil from the case of drawing supplies she always carried around in her bag.

When she lived in California, Cordelia had often spent entire afternoons filling page after page in her sketchbook, but there had been little time for drawing since the ghosts of Shadow School had taken over her life. Now that she was being given the opportunity to create something, she felt a thrum of excitement buzz through her fingertips.

What should I draw?

Answering this question was usually the most difficult part of the process for her. The world, after all, was infinitely drawable, and there were so many things she itched to capture.

Today, however, the answer came quickly.

The gardener.

Leaning so close to the paper that the tips of her hair grazed the table, Cordelia drew like a girl possessed, visualizing the face of the ghost in order to reproduce him on the page. Wrinkled skin. Straw hat. A slash of angry lips. When she was done, she leaned back to review her work. *Not bad—but the eyes are a little off.* She erased them and tried to picture the gardener's reaction when she'd given him the seed: anger, yes, but also fear at the thought of going into his Bright. It was this fear that Cordelia had failed to capture—probably because she couldn't understand how someone could be afraid of their own personal paradise.

She was just beginning to redraw the second eye when a burst of laughter broke her concentration.

Cordelia looked up in annoyance and saw that

Viviana—the pretty girl Benji had been walking with the first day of school—was sitting directly across from her. At some point, she had joined their table and pulled her seat so close to Benji's that their knees were practically touching. Benji didn't seem to mind.

Viviana laughed again, covering her mouth with two hands.

"What's so funny?" Cordelia asked, forcing a smile to her face.

"Benji's drawing," Viviana said. She turned his paper in Cordelia's direction, revealing a confusing mishmash of lines, smudges, and erasure marks. "What do you think this is? Best guess."

Cordelia hesitated, not wanting to be mean. Benji excelled at sports, writing, and cooking—but he could barely draw a stick figure.

"A windmill?" Cordelia suggested.

"A cloud?" tried Agnes, squinting as she looked at the drawing. "A cloud on a . . . stick? A lolli-cloud?"

Benji reached for the paper, but Viviana, now laughing harder than ever, playfully pushed him away. Two girls at a nearby table glanced in their direction and shared a knowing smile. Cordelia was sure that by the end of the day there would be plenty of rumors about Benji and Viviana, if they hadn't started already.

"This is the tree in front of my house!" Benji said, finally snatching the paper from Viviana's hands. "Obviously."

"The big elm?" Viviana asked. "Seriously? That's what you were going for?"

Cordelia looked at her with surprise.

"You've been to Benji's house?" she asked, putting her pencil down. Her strokes had become darker than she intended, and she didn't want to ruin the drawing. "I didn't realize you guys were so close."

"We're not," Viviana said with a mock look of disgust. "I totally hate him. But my mom started working with Benji's mom this summer, and now they're besties and get our families together for pizza nights–"

"Which means I get stuck hanging out with Vivi way too much," Benji said. "Ruined my entire summer, to be honest."

Vivi–not Viviana, Cordelia thought, straining hard to maintain her smile. *How precious.*

"You're just mad because I always kick your butt at *Super Smash*," Vivi said.

"Only because I let you use the good controller."

"Fine. How about we try it at my house next time? See what happens?"

"You're on, Martínez. Just try not to cry when I beat you."

Their banter continued for a few more minutes. Cordelia, who might as well have been invisible, watched their interaction with a stunned expression.

"What's the deal?" she whispered to Agnes. "Benji didn't even know this girl existed last year, and now they're acting like best friends."

Agnes shrugged awkwardly. She didn't like any sort of conflict, particularly between her friends.

"Vivi's really nice once you get to know her," she said.

"*You've* hung out with her too?"

"Just once or twice at Benji's house," Agnes said quietly. She looked down and colored the bill of the platypus she had drawn. "Benji invited you both times, but all you wanted to do was sit in your room and look up ghost stuff."

Cordelia started to argue then remembered that Agnes was right. Benji *had* invited her. *Did you think he was just going to sit in his house alone if you didn't go?* Cordelia wondered, feeling stupid.

"Why does he like her so much?" Cordelia asked. "She can't even see the ghosts!"

Agnes stopped coloring and gave Cordelia a look.

"Neither can I," she said. "Does that mean we should stop being friends?"

"No," Cordelia replied, grimacing. "I'm sorry. That

was a stupid thing to say."

"No worries," Agnes said with a mischievous smile. "You're not thinking rationally. Jealousy will do that to you."

"I'm not jealous," Cordelia said.

Agnes's smile grew wider.

"I'm *not*," Cordelia insisted. "I'm just surprised, that's all."

"Surprised that another girl would want to hang out with Benji, despite the fact that he's cute and nice and funny? Makes total sense."

Cordelia picked up her pencil. "He's not *that* cute," she muttered.

For the rest of the period, she tried to concentrate on her drawing, but her attention kept wandering to Benji and Vivi. By the time the bell rang, she still hadn't gotten the gardener's eyes right. She crumpled up the paper and tossed it in the recycling bin.

8

The House in the Attic

Cordelia got to school early the next day, determined to finally tell Dr. Roqueni that she had broken the architectural model. After peeking into the principal's office and seeing that it was empty, she ran up to the third floor and entered the secret passageway in the storage room. Passing beneath the black pyramids, Cordelia felt a tingle of untapped power, like summer air just before a lightning storm.

She pushed open the trapdoor and climbed into the attic.

It was a dreary day outside, and only a trickle of light shone through the dormer windows. Before knocking on the door to Dr. Roqueni's apartment, Cordelia decided to take a look at the damage to the model house. She was a virtuoso when it came to any sort of arts-and-crafts project, and coming clean would be a lot easier if there was a genuine possibility that she could repair the hole herself.

The moment she saw the house, however, her mouth dropped open. She circled it, running her hand along the back of the roof, sure that there was some sort of mistake.

It was already fixed.

The door to Dr. Roqueni's apartment opened, and the principal stepped into the attic.

"Uncle Darius patched it up before he left," she said. "He has his faults, but even I'll admit that he's a master carpenter. It was tricky to find roof slates that matched the original, but we tracked them down eventually."

"I'm the one who broke it," Cordelia said, blinking away tears. "I'm so sorry."

Dr. Roqueni crossed the room and hugged her. It surprised Cordelia, since the principal wasn't really the hugging type, but it definitely made her feel better.

"I should have told you," Cordelia said.

"You just did," Dr. Roqueni replied. "And you would have told me even earlier if I hadn't sent you home for the summer. I'm sure that was difficult for you, but I really do think it was for the best. There's more to life than just ghosts, Cordelia."

"You sound like Benji," she said, but mentioning his name only made her think of Vivi and her stupid perfect hair, so Cordelia quickly changed the subject. "Elijah sure investigated a lot of haunted houses. Mr. Shadow said that his grandma used to tell him stories about them when he was a kid."

Dr. Roqueni nodded with a grim smile. "He told me those same stories when I was a girl," she said.

"Cool!" Cordelia gestured toward the house she had broken. "Did he tell you about the ghost that haunted this place?"

Dr. Roqueni froze for a moment. Then, slowly, she leaned toward Cordelia and tapped her fingernails on the roof of the house. "Why do"–*tap*–"you"–*tap, tap*–"want to know?" she asked. There was a cold look in her eyes that Cordelia had never seen before.

"Just . . . curious," Cordelia stammered, unsure what she had said to make Dr. Roqueni so upset. "Since I broke it. You don't have to tell me if you don't want to."

The look in Dr. Roqueni's eyes passed. "Sorry," she said, massaging her forehead with two fingers. "I don't like to talk about these houses. My uncle's stories gave me terrible nightmares when I was a kid. He never considered the idea that ghost stories might terrify a little girl."

"Maybe he thought you loved them as much as he did," Cordelia suggested.

"My uncle doesn't *love* the ghosts," Dr. Roqueni said. "He only cares about proving they exist, and that it was Elijah's genius that trapped them here. In his mind, he's on a noble quest to elevate the Shadow name to its rightful place alongside Einstein and Da Vinci. The only thing that's kept him from telling the world about archimancy is the fact that no one would believe him."

"I'm surprised he believes in ghosts himself," Cordelia said. "It's not like he can see them."

"And there's nothing that bothers him more," Dr. Roqueni said with a satisfied smirk. "Even when I was a little girl, he resented the fact that I had the Sight and he didn't. I think that's why he made me work so hard. Every day after school. Every Saturday. Every Sunday." Dr. Roqueni glanced over at the old ghost sitting on the chest, still tapping his foot soundlessly against the floor. "While my friends were out playing in the sun, I searched the darkness for his precious ghosts."

"Is that why you don't want him to know that I have the Sight?" Cordelia asked. "Are you worried he'll try to do the same thing to me?"

Dr. Roqueni nodded. "He knows I won't help him. Not anymore. But if he finds out that you can see the ghosts, he'll try to get your help instead."

"That doesn't sound so bad," Cordelia said. "It might be kind of cool if people knew the truth."

Dr. Roqueni gave her a disappointed look. Cordelia looked down, feeling like one of the bad kids sent to her office.

"There's nothing more dangerous than knowledge," Dr. Roqueni said. "That's why we must keep the ghosts, and Elijah's research, a secret. We don't want the wrong people to figure out how to build a haunted house. They might not have the ghosts' best interests at heart like we do."

"I won't tell anyone," Cordelia said. "But your uncle is going to be pretty ticked off if he ever finds out you've been hiding Elijah's office from him."

"Which is why it'll have to be our little secret," Dr. Roqueni said with a wink. "Listen, I know Darius seems like this sweet old man, but that's just an act so people underestimate him. His age is like a mask he wears to hide his true intentions." Dr. Roqueni glanced at her watch and grimaced. "I'd love to keep chatting, but I have a lot of work to catch up on. With all these after-school meetings, I've been falling behind on everything else."

"Can't you just cancel all the meetings?" Cordelia asked. "You're the boss!"

Dr. Roqueni lowered her brows, as though giving

the idea honest consideration, then winced and rubbed her left temple.

"Are you okay?" Cordelia asked.

"Just a headache," Dr. Roqueni said. "Nothing to worry about. Are you staying after school today? I've seen a few new arrivals who could use your assistance."

"Why bother?" Cordelia asked with a defeated shrug. "The dehaunter is going to free all the ghosts anyway."

"It might," Dr. Roqueni said. "It might not. But either way, you can help the ghosts today. It's not fair to keep them waiting." She crouched in front of the old man sitting on the chest and gazed at him with sympathetic eyes. "Ghosts are cursed to exist among the living, even though they no longer belong in that world. Can you imagine what that's like? Trapped in a house, unable to do anything other than watch, while the living—who are free to come and go as they please—eat and talk and grow old."

Cordelia looked at the old man, wondering what he might be thinking at that very moment, and felt a deep sadness well up inside her. "You're right," she said, promising herself that she would return with the old man's Brightkey soon.

"I knew you'd understand," Dr. Roqueni said, clapping a hand on her shoulder. "You have a good heart,

Cordelia. Now go offer some ghosts their Brightkeys. We're counting on you."

After her talk with Dr. Roqueni, Cordelia felt invigorated. *The ghosts still need me*, she thought. *Besides, who knows if this dehaunter will even work?*

She bounded down the attic stairs two at a time. School wasn't over yet, but Cordelia felt like she was going to burst if she didn't free a spirit right there and then, so she took a left toward the western wing. There were no classrooms here, and she didn't pass a single student. Although Dr. Roqueni had warned them not to free ghosts while school was in session, Cordelia thought this might be an exception.

It's not fair to keep them waiting—that's what she told me.

Cordelia passed beneath a large arch and entered the mirror gallery. There were dozens of them lining a huge open area, their reflective surfaces concealed by billowing black curtains. Cordelia had learned to find beauty in even the darkest corners of Shadow School—the display case of porcelain dolls tucked away in a third-floor cul-de-sac, the rusty tricycle that could be found in a new place every morning—but the mirrors still made her nervous. The worst of them stood three times the height of Cordelia herself, its frame a labyrinth of black pipes topped by a chimney-like cylinder that nearly touched the ceiling. Its curtain was red, not black. Although Cordelia had peeked behind most of the curtains that guarded the mirrors, she had never touched that one. Even her insatiable curiosity had its limits.

She walked past the ghost she called Hopeless Bob—an ordinary-looking man whose generic appearance seemed to offer no clues to his Brightkey. There were a dozen other ghosts just like him spread throughout the school. They had been there even longer than Cordelia, and she had no idea how to help them.

"Someday, Bob," Cordelia offered. "We'll figure it out."

The droopy-faced ghost didn't seem to share her optimism.

Just past the mirror gallery was a ghost in her late teens. Both arms were weighted down with shopping bags, as though she had just come from the mall. Cordelia could see printing on the bags, where the names of the stores would normally go, but the letters were blurry and impossible to read.

"I get it," Cordelia told the ghost. "Before I moved here, I used to live for shopping too. But now that I know about you guys, I can't get as into it. It's hard to buy a new pair of shoes when I can use that money on Brightkeys instead."

She remembered how she had dragged her poor parents all over Union Square, begging for the right shoes or the perfect bag, and felt a flush of embarrassment. *I could have been this girl,* she thought, suddenly feeling as though she were looking at a different sort of ghost—the ghost of what might have been.

Cordelia took out the expired credit card she had found in a kitchen drawer and laid it on the ground. The ghost didn't hesitate. She picked it up with an eager look in her eyes, and a black triangle appeared above her. It started to open. Cordelia heard mall music and the computerized beeps of items being scanned for purchase. The ghost inhaled deeply, like a sailor smelling the ocean breeze.

Then she flung the credit card away.

Unlike the gardener, this ghost wasn't angry. She watched the triangle vanish with desperate longing but also fear, as though her Bright were a temptation that needed to be resisted at all costs.

When it finally closed, the ghost looked very pleased with herself.

"What's the matter with you?" Cordelia asked. "Why don't you want to leave?"

The ghost dropped her shopping bags, which dematerialized into confetti before vanishing completely. She

77

then pinched her nose, like a swimmer about to dive into deep water, and leaped high into the air. Her downward progress was slowed—but not stopped—by the floor, making it look as though she were riding an invisible elevator. After the rest of her body had descended out of sight, the ghost poked her hand through the floor and gave Cordelia one final wave goodbye.

9

Vivi's Party

School settled into its familiar routines. Tests were given. Class pictures taken. Friendships forged. October snuck up on them with a sucker punch of cold New England air, sending parents scurrying for winter clothes that had been stored for later in the year.

Cordelia settled into a routine of her own, rescuing ghosts in the mornings and occasionally staying after school when there wasn't a faculty meeting. On most days, she worked alone. Benji usually had soccer practice, and even when he did join her, he spent a lot of time checking his phone. Agnes had stopped rescuing ghosts entirely so she could concentrate on the dehaunter. Cordelia still had reservations about the machine, but what could she really say? It wasn't like things were going so great with the Brightkeys. A growing number of ghosts were tossing them away at the last minute and vanishing soon afterward.

Cordelia wondered where they had gone.

Since Agnes would be visiting her dad in Boston, Cordelia planned on spending Halloween at home, handing out candy to the neighborhood kids. With only a few days to spare, however, Benji offered an alternate plan: Viviana was throwing a party at her house, and they were both invited. Cordelia was reluctant at first, but Benji finally convinced her to go. Since there weren't many options left at the costume store, Cordelia settled on black leggings, a makeup stick that she could use to draw a nose and whiskers, and pointy cat ears. It was better than nothing.

At six o'clock, Mr. and Mrs. Núñez drove them to Vivi's house, a modest split-level at the end of a dark road. Cordelia could hear music inside. Several jack-o'-lanterns with lopsided grins sat on the front steps.

Cordelia tugged at the sleeve of Benji's soccer jersey. "How is this a costume again?"

"I told you. I'm Dave. And he's me."

"And I would know this because . . ."

Benji pointed to his back. "This is number ten! That's Dave's number. I'm number twelve!" He sighed with frustration. "Everyone at the party will get it—there're going to be a ton of soccer kids. Vivi's the goalie for the girls' team. She's awesome!"

"Of course she is," Cordelia muttered.

Benji rang the doorbell. A bubbly woman who Cordelia assumed was Mrs. Martínez shrieked with joy and wrapped Benji in a huge hug.

"*¿No te ves guapo? ¡Viviana! ¡Tu novio está aquí!*"

Color bloomed in Benji's cheeks.

"What did she say?" Cordelia asked.

"Nothing," Benji said, clearly not wanting to tell her.

Several other adults, all speaking Spanish at once, rushed to greet Benji. A man wearing a wizard hat slung an arm around his shoulders as though he were part of the family and led him deeper into the house. The others followed.

Cordelia was left alone in the foyer.

"No problem," she said. "I'll just, you know, find my way to the party. It's cool."

She started toward the sound of music, but before she had taken three steps Vivi bounded into the room. Cordelia's heart plummeted.

They were wearing the same costume.

81

"Cat power," Vivi said with a smile, giving her a hug. Cordelia caught a whiff of perfume. "You look so cute."

"You too," Cordelia said.

Except Vivi didn't look cute. She looked amazing. Compared to her, Cordelia felt like a scrawny, one-eared tomcat that dumpster-dived in alleyways.

"My family stole Benji, didn't they?" Vivi asked with a grin. "He's kind of a rock star around here. I'll have to rescue him later. Come on, I'll take you downstairs."

They passed the kitchen, where an older woman wearing an apron was frying plantains, and continued through a small den. Dozens of trophies lined the shelves.

"Are these all yours?" Cordelia asked.

Vivi rolled her eyes. "Sorry. I keep telling my dad to stick these somewhere else, but he's a little extra when it comes to sports. I've been playing soccer since I was big enough to kick the ball."

"Don't you like it?"

Vivi looked surprised by the question, as though she had never considered it before. "It's what I do," she said. "How about you? You play any sports?"

"I can throw a Frisbee sort of straight. That's about it."

"How about boys?"

"How about them?"

"Is there someone you like?" Vivi asked. It was a casual, do-we-have-math-homework-tonight sort of tone, but her smile was nervous. "I promise I won't tell anyone."

Benji, Cordelia thought. *She wants to know if I'm into Benji.*

Cordelia hesitated, unsure how to respond now that she had decoded Vivi's reason for asking. In the end, she decided to stick with the truth.

"I have too many other things on my mind right now to think about boys," Cordelia said.

"Like what?" Vivi asked, unable to hide the look of relief in her eyes.

Cordelia shrugged. "School stuff."

They went into the basement, which was packed with kids. Most of them were sitting on the floor or in foldable plastic chairs, playing with their phones. Mason James and his crew were killing zombies on the TV. Only a few people had bothered to wear a costume.

Benji waved in their direction, and Vivi cut through the crowd and gave him a quick, awkward hug. Cordelia wondered if he liked her perfume. Within moments, a group of kids brushed past Cordelia as though she wasn't there and formed a circle around Benji and Vivi. Many were wearing blue soccer jerseys with

LUDLOW BOBCATS emblazoned across the front. Cordelia had never spoken to any of them, but she knew their names. Benji talked about his teammates a lot.

"Cool party," a boy named Aaron O'Sullivan told Vivi. He was a rail-thin eighth grader who always seemed to be snacking on something; right now it was handful of Skittles. "Kelly said she'll drop by later. Her parents are making her go trick-or-treating with her little sister first."

"Lame," said Lizzie Blevins. A single AirPod dangled from her ear like a misplaced earring. "I'm so glad I don't have any brothers or sisters."

"What about Eric?" Benji asked.

"He doesn't count," replied Lizzie.

"You guys are so lucky you didn't have practice today," Vivi told the boys. "Ms. Simmons kept us until five. I barely had time to get ready for the party."

"We were supposed to scrimmage, but Mr. Bruce had another headache," said Dave Gagnon, a stocky midfielder wearing sports goggles. "He canceled it at the last minute."

"Ms. Patel was complaining about a headache during class yesterday," said Aaron. "Must be a teacher virus or something."

"Nice," said Lizzie. "Maybe they'll all be absent on Monday."

"Don't say that," said Vivi. "I like our teachers."

"You like everyone," said Lizzie. An accusation, not a compliment.

"I actually dropped by the gym after school to ask Mr. Bruce if practice was going to be canceled tomorrow," said Dave. "I thought he might have gone home early, because the lights were off, but he was still there."

Dave's voice grew softer, and the group gathered around him in a tight huddle. Cordelia stood on her tiptoes in order to peek over Lizzie's shoulder.

"It was freaky," Dave continued. "Mr. Bruce was just walking from one side of the gym to the other. Only he wasn't walking normal. More like stumbling."

"He was totally drunk," Lizzie said with an eager smile.

"That's not funny," Vivi said. "And don't start spreading any rumors. Mr. Bruce just has the flu or something."

Cordelia knew that Vivi was probably right. Winter was around the corner, and the teachers had been spending a lot of time together during their meetings. It made logical sense that a few of them, including Dr. Roqueni, had gotten sick.

Then why didn't Mr. Bruce just go home? Why hang out in the gym, walking back and forth in the dark?

If Cordelia had attended another school, she

probably would have let it go. But this was Shadow School. The logical explanation wasn't always the right one.

"Did you notice anything else that was odd?" she asked Dave, who looked startled that a nonsoccer person was speaking to him. "Did the gym lights start flickering on and off? Was it colder than usual? Did you hear–"

"Hey," said Aaron, looking back and forth from Dave to Benji. "Did you guys switch jerseys?"

"Yeah!" Benji exclaimed, thrilled that someone had noticed. "We're being each other for Halloween!"

"Awesome!"

This was followed by an epic series of high fives that involved hands, elbows, and feet. By the time they were done, no one seemed to recall that Cordelia had been talking. She wandered over to the snack table and ladled punch into a cup, dodging the plastic eyeballs bobbing to the surface. From the corner of her eye, she saw a boy with extremely pale skin standing in the corner. She spun around with her first real smile of the night, hoping to see a ghost, but it was just Grant Thompson. He had been sick all week.

Cordelia checked the time. Only three hours and forty minutes to go.

She took a seat on the couch next to a figure wearing

a white sheet with eyeholes. Somehow, he or she was still managing to send a text.

"Is it okay if I sit here for a while?" Cordelia asked.

The ghost nodded.

Settling into her seat, Cordelia drank her punch and thought about her conversation with Dr. Roqueni. *Ghosts are cursed to exist among the living, even though they no longer belong in that world. Can you imagine what that's like?*

Cordelia thought she could.

10

Window Room

Cordelia stepped off the bus Monday morning and saw Darius Shadow sitting on a bench outside the school. He was holding the brass key that usually hung from his neck and staring at it with a thoughtful expression. Cordelia froze, unsure what to do. Dr. Roqueni had warned her to keep her distance, but what harm could come from saying hello? He was just an old man, and he looked so sad, sitting there all alone.

I'll just stop for a second to make sure he's okay, Cordelia decided. *Then I'll head straight inside.*

"Good morning, Mr. Shadow," she said.

Darius looked up at her and smiled. "Ahh," he said. "My friend from the attic! We meet again!"

"My name's Cordelia," she said.

Darius whistled, impressed. "That's quite a moniker," he said. "I don't believe I've ever met a Cordelia before."

"My parents got it from a Shakespeare play. I hated it when I was a little girl. But I don't mind it so much anymore."

"Good," Darius said. "You should be proud of the name your folks gave you. Besides, there are enough Elizabeths and Katies in the world. Cordelia's unique. It suits you."

Darius turned the brass key in his weathered hands. The key had a long shaft and decorative bow, like something you might find in the antique shops Cordelia's dad sometimes dragged her to on rainy Sundays. A black leather cord, knotted at one end so it could be worn around the neck, dangled from the key like a tail.

"What does it open?" Cordelia asked.

"Nothing anymore," Darius said. "But that doesn't mean it isn't valuable. This was the key to the very first house that Elijah Shadow built. After his beloved wife, Hallie, died, he couldn't bear living there anymore. But he saved the key and gave it to their daughter, Wilma."

"The one who told you ghost stories when you were a kid," Cordelia said, taking a seat next to him on the bench.

"You remembered," Darius said with a grin. "Grandma Wilma wore it every day of her life and gifted it to me on her deathbed. Not my sister. Not my brother. Me. She knew who really loved the Shadow family." He pinched the key tightly between his fingers. "When there's a museum built to honor Elijah's contributions to the world, this key will sit in a huge display case right in the front entrance. Millions of people will come to see it!"

As Darius spoke about his imaginary museum, an obsessive gleam swept over his eyes. It was the look of a man who wouldn't let anything stand in his way. For a moment, Cordelia understood why Dr. Roqueni felt her uncle was dangerous. Then the moment passed, and Darius turned to her and smiled, looking once more like a harmless old man. He looped the black cord over his neck, restoring the key to its usual position next to his heart.

"Looks like November's been born with a full set of teeth this year," Darius said, rubbing his hands together for warmth. "Never could get used to the weather up here. These old bones were made for the sun."

"It's not so bad once you get used to it," Cordelia said, realizing that she should get to class. "Should I let Dr. Roqueni know you're here?"

"She already knows. I knocked on her office door

not ten minutes ago. Alas, she wasn't too keen to see me. When I refused to leave, she asked a few of her teachers to escort me out the door."

"Seriously?" Cordelia asked. She knew Dr. Roqueni didn't trust her uncle, but kicking him out seemed a little harsh. "Is she mad at you or something?"

"Aria is always mad at me," Darius said, hanging his head low. "And I can't say I blame her. When she was just a girl, I didn't always have her best interests at heart."

"Have you told her you're sorry?"

Darius unleashed a bitter laugh. "More times than I can count," he said. "But I guess she still has trouble believing me when I say I'm worried about her."

"Worried about her?" Cordelia asked. "Why?"

"It might be nothing," Darius said. "But during my visit this summer, Aria was acting strange. She refused to leave the school and kept complaining that her head hurt. And then one time, I woke up in the middle of the night to use the bathroom, and Aria was staring at the mirror, making faces." Darius gave an exaggerated smile, then wiped a hand over his face and frowned. "Like an actor practicing for a part."

A cold breeze kicked up a pile of leaves by the curb. Cordelia watched them skitter across the pavement.

"Dr. Roqueni's been working hard lately," Cordelia

said, trying to make sense of what Darius was telling her. "Lots of teacher meetings. I know when my mom's stressed out she gets migraines and can't sleep, so maybe it's like that."

"Maybe," Darius said, but she could tell he didn't really believe it. He pulled out his wallet and handed Cordelia a business card. "Could you do me a favor and keep an eye on her? Call me if you notice anything unusual. Or just shoot me a text. I'm not *that* old."

Cordelia stared down at the card. It was cream colored with Darius's name and phone number printed in an elegant font. She wanted to believe that Darius was just concerned about his niece. But it was strange that he was offering his phone number to a twelve-year-old.

Remember what Dr. Roqueni said, she thought. *You can't trust him.*

"Sorry," Cordelia said, trying to return the card. "But I don't know how I can help. I barely see Dr. Roqueni."

"My apologies," Darius said. "I assumed that since you were helping my niece this summer, you might be a particular favorite of hers. I know teachers and principals aren't supposed to have favorites, of course. But they're only human. It happens. Especially if the adult and child have similar . . . interests."

He gave her a knowing smile. *You can see ghosts*, his

eyes seemed to say. *Why don't you just admit it?*

Cordelia kept her expression blank and shook her head.

"Dr. Roqueni is the principal. I'm a student. That's all there is to it."

A fleeting look of disappointment passed over Darius's face.

"Well, keep your eyes open, just in case," he said, rising to his feet. "You seem like an unusually observant child. In fact, I bet you see all sorts of things that no one else does."

As Darius shuffled his way across the parking lot, Cordelia realized that his card was still in her hand. She considered tossing it into a trash can, then stuffed it into her pocket instead. She didn't know exactly why.

On their way to first period, Cordelia told Benji and Agnes about her encounter with Darius Shadow.

"Why does he think that you can see ghosts?" Benji asked.

Agnes rolled her eyes. "He found you guys in a dark attic, in a haunted school, in the summer," she said. "It wouldn't take a dendrochronologist to figure it out."

"A den-what?" Benji asked.

"Dendrochronologist. They study tree rings. It's a lot harder than it sounds."

"Mr. Shadow definitely has his suspicions about me," Cordelia said. "Probably you too, Benj. But as long as we keep playing dumb, there's no way for him to know for sure."

"Good," Benji said. "I don't trust that guy."

"He's not so bad," replied Cordelia. "And he definitely cares about Dr. Roqueni. He's worried about her."

"Because she made some funny faces in a mirror?" Benji asked. "Big deal. My little sisters do that all the time."

"Your sisters are seven," Cordelia said. "It's a little different. Also—remember what your friend Dave said about Mr. Bruce? How he was walking back and forth across the gym in the dark?"

"What about it?"

"Well, that's *weird*. Just like Dr. Roqueni looking in the mirror. And they both had headaches—Ms. Patel too. That has to be more than just a coincidence. We should look into it."

Cordelia watched her friends exchange a dubious look. Clearly, they weren't seeing it.

"My aunt is a teacher," Benji said. "She says her students give her headaches all the time. We actually get her a giant bottle of Tylenol every year for Christmas." He chuckled to himself. "And a cheese grater, but that's another story."

94

"I'm with Benji on this one," said Agnes. "This is Shadow School. If the teachers weren't acting odd, it would be . . . odd. I'm sure it's nothing."

"I guess," Cordelia said.

She knew her friends were probably right, but she was bummed that they weren't more curious. At the very least, she had hoped to bat around a few theories, just like old times.

They're too busy thinking about the dehaunter, she thought. *Well, Agnes is. Benji's probably thinking about Vivi.*

They entered Ms. Jackson's science classroom. It had the number 313 outside its door, but everyone just called it the Window Room. It was easy to see why: The walls were jigsaw-puzzled together out of windows that varied in shape, size, and style, without an inch of drywall between them. As if this wasn't odd enough, not a single window looked upon the outside world; instead of staring at trees or clouds, bored students could watch the comings and goings in the hallway, or make faces at the kids in the adjoining classrooms. Like the second-floor staircase that looped back on itself or the goblin-sized door in the ceiling of Mr. Hearn's room, the windows were there for reasons only Elijah Shadow understood, a necessary part of the architectural magic that drew spirits to the school and kept them from leaving.

Cordelia, Benji, and Agnes took their seats at one of the tall, old-fashioned lab tables. Ms. Jackson—who had curly brown hair and could have been mistaken for a high school student—stood just behind them. Each time a new student entered, she shrank deeper into the back corner of the room. Cordelia heard her mumble: "Nothing to be scared of. It's just like you practiced last night, only with a bunch of kids staring at you." Ms. Jackson closed her eyes and inhaled deeply. "Forty-eight little eyes. Watching every single move you make. Judging you . . ."

"She seems even more nervous than usual today," Benji whispered. "Maybe it's because Agnes corrected her like five hundred times yesterday."

"It was only seven," Agnes insisted. "And I was very polite about it."

At last, Ms. Jackson found the courage to begin the class. "Today we're going to learn about cell structure," she said, her voice so quiet that Cordelia had to lean forward just to hear her. "It's truly fascinating. Each cell is like a tiny little organism hidden inside our bodies. There's the nucleus, which is the brain. And the cytoskeleton, which is like a body. And, of course, the . . . the . . ."

She stared at the class, her face blank, like an actress who had forgotten her lines. Mason whispered something to the other kids at his table and they burst into laughter, which rattled Ms. Jackson further.

"Cilium?" Agnes suggested helpfully. "Lysosome? Mitochondrion?"

Ms. Jackson wiped the sweat from her forehead, cleared her throat twice—and ran out of the room.

"You scared her off," Benji said to Agnes.

"I didn't mean to! Should I run after her?"

"I'm sure she'll come back eventually," Cordelia said, though she thought it was equally possible that Ms. Jackson might run out the front doors of Shadow School and never return. "In the meantime, maybe we can try to figure out why all these ghosts have been turning down their—"

"Oh!" Agnes exclaimed. "That reminds me. There's something I wanted to show you." She dug through her backpack and retrieved a leather-bound journal, turning her body to shield it from the other students (who had all started conversations of their own). "I read a few of Elijah's journals on the train ride to Boston and learned some cool stuff. You remember last year how Dr. Roqueni told us there were super-rare people who could see ghosts everywhere, not just Shadow School? Elijah was one of those people."

"I wondered about that," Cordelia said. "Guess that's how he was able to tell how all those houses were haunted. He could see the ghosts."

"Except he did more than just see them," Agnes said. "If they were causing problems, he actually got rid of them."

"Cool," Benji said, half listening. The majority of his attention was focused on Vivi, who was waving at him to join her table.

Cordelia smacked him in the arm.

"Ow!"

"Pay attention," Cordelia said.

"Elijah didn't get rid of the ghosts for free," Agnes continued after giving them both an amused smile. She flipped through the pages of the journal. "Not usually, at least. The owner had to pay him first. Check this out. There's actually a price list."

She held the page open while Cordelia and Agnes read it:

Spirit (child) . . . . *Free*
Spirit (animal) . . . . *$15 per attempt*
Spirit (nonviolent human) . . . . . *$40 per attempt*
Spirit (violent human) . . . . *$70 per attempt*
Poltergeist . . . . *$125 per attempt*
Phantom . . . . *To be determined
on a case-by-case basis*

"That's it?" Benji asked. "I would have charged a lot more than that."

"This was a long time ago," Agnes said. "Forty dollars then would be like a thousand dollars today."

"Not bad," Benji said, nodding in admiration.

Cordelia placed her finger on the bottom of the list. "What does this mean?" she asked. "'Phantom?'"

"I knew you'd ask about that," Agnes said. "Apparently when some ghosts got old—like, really old—they changed. Sometimes they developed special abilities. Like Elijah himself. He probably didn't become a poltergeist until he had been dead for a long time. But sometimes the changes were more horrific. In his journal, Elijah wrote about seeing spirits that barely looked human anymore. He called them phantoms. They were so dangerous that even regular ghosts were scared of them."

Benji's face turned pale. "I am so glad you finished that dehaunter," he said.

"You finished it?" Cordelia asked in disbelief. "The dehaunter? It's done?"

"You didn't tell her?" Benji asked.

"Sorry," Agnes said, blushing. "It's just, every time I talk about the dehaunter, you go all scrunchy face."

Cordelia furrowed her brows.

"That face!" Agnes exclaimed. "Right there!"

"It's a little scrunchy," Benji agreed.

"Sorry," Cordelia said. "But I just think that before we do any dehaunting, we should figure out why these ghosts have suddenly decided they're not interested in their Brights anymore. Aren't you curious?"

Benji shook his head. "The only thing I'm curious about is what it'll be like to walk through these hallways and not have to wonder, 'Hmm . . . is that dude a new teacher? Or a new dead guy?'" He slipped down from his stool and patted his hair into place. "I'm going to say hi to a few people. I'll be back."

By "a few people," Benji meant Vivi, of course. There were no available seats at her table, but she quickly grabbed an unoccupied stool and set it by her side. Benji hopped on it eagerly, and the two jumped into an animated conversation.

"Benji's right, you know," Agnes said. "If this dehaunter works, it doesn't matter if the ghosts are acting weird or not. They'll all be set free. Isn't that what you want?"

"Of course," Cordelia said.

For the most part, she was telling the truth—more than anything else, she wanted to save the ghosts. And yet, there was a small, selfish part of her that wanted the ghosts to stay. Cordelia *liked* saving them, and she was worried about how things might change once the ghosts were no longer a part of her life.

Will I ever find something I love as much as helping them? she wondered. *And will Benji and Agnes want to stay friends with me afterward?*

There was no way to know for sure.

After spending the rest of science deep in conversation (until Ms. Jackson finally returned with ten minutes left in the period), Benji and Vivi walked together to their next class, shoulders practically touching as Agnes and a grim-faced Cordelia trailed behind them. They made sure they were on the same volleyball team at gym—Benji serving up perfect bump passes that Vivi smashed over the net—shared a plate of french fries at lunch, and chose seats at the same table during art and social studies. For the first time ever, Cordelia was excited for math, since Mrs. Machen never let the students pick their own seats—but in some ways, this ended up being even worse. Every time Cordelia glanced over at Benji, he was craning his neck in order to get Vivi's attention from the other side of the room—or maybe just to catch a glimpse of her.

It was enough to make you sick.

Finally, Cordelia couldn't take it anymore. She asked to use the pass and wandered down to the first floor with no particular destination in mind, just wanting to get away from Benji and Vivi as quickly as possible. Agnes thought Cordelia was jealous, which was ridiculous—she had no interest in dating right now. Yes, she had noticed that Benji was kind of cute, but only in a passing way, like when her mom commented on a nice house. It was natural to notice, but that didn't mean they were house shopping. Right now, she had more important things on her mind than flirty texts and holding hands in a movie theater.

The ghosts came first.

That being said, thinking about the stupid smile Benji seemed to get whenever he talked to Vivi made her stomach hurt. Cordelia didn't want to date Benji—at least, not yet—but she didn't want anyone else to date him, either. Could you reserve a boy like a book at the library?

She heard someone call her name.

"Hello?" she asked, looking around. The hallway was silent and empty.

"Cordelia," a voice whispered. "Is he gone?"

She spotted a pair of scared eyes peeking from behind a partially open door.

"Hey, Ezra," Cordelia said, recognizing the boy she had met on the first day of school. "Whatcha doing?"

"Hiding," he said. "I was coming back from Dr.

Roqueni's office when I saw that boy who was picking on me the first day of school. He was looking down at his phone, but I didn't want to take any chances, so I hid."

"The coast is clear," Cordelia said. "By now, Mason is probably on the other side of the school, pulling the wings off flies or kicking a puppy."

"You're funny," Ezra said, stepping into the hallway.

"I've always thought so," Cordelia said.

Ezra was wearing blue corduroy pants, a pink button-down shirt, and a polka-dot bow tie. *His parents aren't doing this poor kid any favors*, she thought.

"Do you think you could walk me back to Mrs. King's room?" he asked. "I'm a little lost."

"My pleasure," Cordelia said. "What were you doing in Dr. Roqueni's office?"

Ezra blushed, setting the freckles on his face aflame.

"Mrs. King sent me there," he said. "I got in trouble for letting Lemonade out of his tank. He looked kind of lonely, so I wanted to hold him for a while. Only he got away, and now we can't find him."

"I'm sure he'll turn up," Cordelia said.

"Dr. Roqueni was really nice about it. She said she didn't think anything should be trapped in a cage, even a gecko, so she appreciated the sentiment."

"That sounds like her," Cordelia said. "Sorry you've had such a rough day."

"It's not as bad as my sixth birthday party, when I threw up all over my cake," Ezra said. "Or my seventh birthday, when my parents wrapped up a pet guinea pig in a box but forgot to make air holes."

"You haven't had much luck with birthdays, have you?"

"I dread them every year."

They walked through an intersection. Out of habit, Cordelia registered that there was a new ghost at the end of the hallway to her left, but she ignored it for now. There wasn't much she could do with Ezra there.

A few steps later, however, she came to an abrupt halt. Something about the ghost was nagging at her—a teasing familiarity.

She backtracked for a closer look. The ghost was heading in the opposite direction, but even from this distance there was no mistaking his distinctive hat and gloves.

The gardener.

"What are you looking at?" Ezra asked, following her gaze. "There's nothing there."

"Shh," Cordelia said, pulling him out of view and holding a finger to her lips. "I have to go. Just keep walking straight, and you'll go right past Mrs. King's room."

Ezra nodded. "Don't take this the wrong way," he

said, "but you're a little weird."

Cordelia couldn't really argue with that, so she gave a brief nod and took off after the gardener, just in time to see him make a left at the end of the hallway. Not only had the gardener escaped his ghost zone, but there seemed to be no limitation to where he could go. She followed him up to the third floor, maintaining her distance in case he looked behind him. At one point the gardener took a shortcut through a wall of lockers, which was hardly fair, but Cordelia was able to pick him up on the other side. His stride was determined and purposeful. Cordelia didn't think this was haunting for haunting's sake. He had a particular destination in mind.

Where are you off to? she wondered.

The bell rang.

Within moments, the hall was packed with students. Cordelia tried to keep following the gardener, but she was moving against the traffic, jostled left and right by a stampede of much bigger kids. A quintet of gossiping girls refused to part, and Cordelia had to press herself against the wall to dodge their moving barricade. By that point, she had lost sight of the gardener altogether. Cordelia grunted in frustration and kicked a locker.

"Everything okay?" Mr. Derleth asked, walking over. His classroom was right across the hall. "You look as if you've seen a . . . well, you know."

"I'm fine," she said. "But there is definitely something weird going on here. Can we meet after school? All of us?"

Mr. Derleth shook his head. "There's a faculty meeting today," he said with an apologetic shrug. "And Dr. Roqueni and I have a lot to do to set up the dehaunter for its test."

"This is important," Cordelia insisted.

"Nothing is more important than the dehaunter," Mr. Derleth said. "But let me talk to Dr. Roqueni. I'm sure we can find a time to meet after the test, if that will make you feel better."

"Why do we have to wait until—"

"Sorry, Cordelia," Mr. Derleth said. "I have to run."

Before she could say another word, Mr. Derleth crossed the hall and entered his classroom. Cordelia noticed him massaging his temples as he closed the door.

11

Test Run

By the following Friday, they were ready to test the dehaunter.

Cordelia, Agnes, and Benji headed up to the mirror gallery immediately after school. The hallways were empty. Dr. Roqueni had canceled all after-school activities and given the entire staff permission to leave as soon as the dismissal bell rang. She didn't want to risk any interruptions.

Agnes paced back and forth as they waited for the adults to arrive. She had been nervous and scatterbrained all day. For once, Ms. Jackson had actually corrected *her*.

"Relax, Agnes," Benji said. His eyes shone with

anticipation, as though he was stepping onto a plane for a long vacation. "This school is about to be ghost free!"

"I'm forgetting something," Agnes said, lifting her spectercles to check a to-do list in her notebook. "I calibrated the dehaunter so it only worked with a single mirror, baked preemptive brownies in case we needed to celebrate . . . uh! The curtains!"

She walked past Hopeless Bob, who looked grateful to have so many visitors for a change, and drew the curtain of the mirror behind him. Dust flew everywhere.

"The dehaunter can't do its thing if the mirror is covered," Agnes said. She grabbed a roll of paper towels and a bottle of Windex from her backpack. "The surface has to be spotless, too."

"Is that why the curtains are there?" Cordelia asked. "To keep the glass from getting dirty?"

"Actually, no," Agnes said. "The curtains are there to keep people from looking into the mirrors. This way they can stay at full strength. Elijah had this theory that each time a mirror cast a reflection it lost a little of its 'inherent mystical power.'"

"Wow," said Cordelia. "And here I thought mirrors were just to show me how bad my hair looked in the morning."

"You could never look bad," Benji said, the words

slipping out of his mouth before he realized what he was saying. "I meant your hair, not you," he added quickly, trying to recover. "Your hair could never look bad. 'Cause it's so short. Like, how messy can it get?"

"Thanks," Cordelia muttered.

Benji snagged the paper towels and Windex from Agnes, who seemed to take great delight in his awkwardness.

"I got this," he said, and began to scrub the mirror. Though his back was facing her, Cordelia could still see Benji's reflection. His cheeks were aflame.

He said I could never look bad, Cordelia thought. *Does that mean he thinks I'm pretty?* The thought made her feel confused and excited in equal measure. *No, that doesn't make sense. Benji is into Vivi. Just because he thinks I never look bad, doesn't mean he thinks I look good. It just means I'm average. And even if he thought I was, maybe, a tiny bit pretty, there's no way I'm in Vivi's league.*

She shook her head, annoyed that her thoughts had wandered so far, and refocused her attention on the more important matter at hand.

"Make sure it's perfect," Agnes told Benji, peeking over his shoulder as he scrubbed the mirror. "Not even a single streak."

"No worries," Benji said. "My mom makes me clean our windows every weekend. I've got pro skills."

He started to whistle, no longer blushing. *This is a big day for him*, Cordelia thought. *For both of them.* She wished she could share her friends' excitement, but there was something about the dehaunter that continued to trouble her. *Just one press of a button and all the ghosts are gone?* she wondered. *It shouldn't be that easy.*

Dr. Roqueni entered the room. She had dressed up for the occasion in an old-fashioned green dress embroidered with black flowers. It wasn't her usual style, but Cordelia thought she looked beautiful.

"Mr. Derleth is waiting in the dehaunter room downstairs," Dr. Roqueni said, looking past the children to fix her hair in the mirror. She regarded Agnes with a cool gaze. "I wanted to confirm that everything was ready to go before telling him to turn it on. There can't be any mistakes tonight."

"We're all set," Agnes replied. "But it might not be such a good idea to stand so close to the mirror. Just in case."

"I thought you said this was safe," Cordelia said.

"I believe the word I used was 'safe-ish,'" Agnes said.

"That's not actually a word."

"Let's err on the side of caution," Dr. Roqueni said, backing away nervously. "We'll be able to see just fine at the other end of the gallery. You have the power set to the lowest possible level, correct?"

"Barely a trickle," Agnes said, nodding. "Still not sure what the dehaunter *does*, exactly. Could turn the mirror into a portal that leads outside. Which would be cool. Or it might make an actual Bright appear, which would be awesome!"

"Does it matter?" Benji asked. "The ghosts are gone either way."

Cordelia saw Dr. Roqueni's lips twitch, as though she were about to disagree. She changed her mind at the last minute, however, and ushered the children to the opposite end of the gallery, where she raised a walkie-talkie to her lips.

"We're ready," she said.

The four of them focused on the mirror behind Hopeless Bob. The ghost glanced behind him, wondering what he was missing.

"Nothing's happening," Dr. Roqueni said, squeezing her hands tightly into fists. "Why isn't anything happening?"

"Give it time," Agnes said, a bead of nervous sweat running down her cheek. "It needs to warm up first. Like my mom's car on a cold morning."

A few moments later there was a sound like water sloshing against the inside of a tin drum, and the reflective surface of the mirror turned black. An invisible force yanked Hopeless Bob toward the mirror. As though reacting to the ghost's presence, the black surface rippled and changed, revealing a playground on a summer evening. Cordelia heard the squeak of swings and children's laughter.

"It's a Bright," she said, eyes wide with astonishment.

She waited for Hopeless Bob to step forward into the playground, but instead the mirror held him in place while it changed again. This time, it revealed a snowy mountaintop.

It's searching for the correct Bright, Cordelia thought, watching in fascination as the mirror continued to switch between locations. Finally, it settled on a perfectly ordinary living room. A small TV sat across from a broken-down easy chair with a strip of duct tape on one arm. Hopeless Bob burst into a glorious smile as he floated through the portal.

The mirror immediately turned black again.

"Shut it down," Dr. Roqueni said into her walkie-talkie.

A few seconds later, the mirror was just a mirror. Benji raised Agnes's arms into the air and shouted, "MVP, MVP!" Cordelia hugged Agnes close. She still wasn't sure how she felt about the dehaunter, but she would figure that out later. Right now, she was just proud of her brilliant best friend.

"You really are a genius," Cordelia whispered in her ear.

Looking over Agnes's shoulder, she noticed Dr. Roqueni crossing the gallery to stand before the mirror, pressing one hand flat against the glass. Her reflection stared back at her with a dour expression. Cordelia was surprised. She expected the principal to be thrilled that the dehaunter had worked, but her face was shrouded with disappointment.

"Dr. Roqueni?" Cordelia called out. "Everything okay?"

In the mirror, Cordelia saw the principal take a deep breath, as though composing herself. When she turned around, there was a big smile on her face.

"Everything's wonderful," she said, folding her hands behind her back. "Our test was a success. The dehaunter works. In a few weeks, we'll be ready to try it for real."

"A few *weeks*?" Benji asked, throwing his hands into the air. "Why wait? Let's send all these ghosts home right now!"

Dr. Roqueni's mouth tightened to a thin line.

"That would be an extremely foolhardy course of action," she said, making her way back across the mirror gallery. "Mr. Derleth and I will need to conduct a full inspection of the dehaunter before moving forward. There may be a few modifications that need to be made before we use it for real."

"Modifications?" Agnes asked. "Like what?"

"I'm not sure," Dr. Roqueni replied. "That's why we need to inspect it. Better safe than sorry."

"I guess that makes sense," Agnes said. "We're playing with a lot of spectral energy here. Like, nuclear-reactor level. It isn't the type of thing you can mess around with."

Benji sighed with resignation. "All right," he said. "I've been stuck with the ghosts since the fifth grade. Guess I can wait a few more weeks. What do you think, Cord?"

"Sounds like a plan," she said, only half listening. Her mind was still trying to make sense of what she had seen in the mirror. *Why had Dr. Roqueni looked so disappointed? Hadn't the dehaunter done exactly what she wanted it to?*

What was she hiding from them?

They were on the verge of freeing all the ghosts of Shadow School. Yet Cordelia's instincts told them they were in more danger than ever.

Mount Washington

Seventh-grade lunch was always crazy loud, but the following Monday it was even worse than usual. Cordelia and her friends had to huddle close just to hear one another.

"First thing I'm going to do when all the ghosts are gone," Benji said through a mouthful of macaroni and cheese, "is walk through every inch of Shadow School and enjoy the fact that no one is watching me do it. Then I'm finally going to try out for this travel team that plays soccer all over New Hampshire. See what it's like to have some real competition for a change. How about you, Ag?"

"It's different for me," she said. "I can't see them, so

it's not that big of a change."

"Come on," Benji said. "There must be something."

Agnes thoughtfully swirled her spoon through her organic yogurt.

"I guess there's this one thing," she said. "It's a year-long STEM program for gifted girls that I've dreamed of joining since I was in first grade. It's taught by real scientists! They only admit ten girls in the entire state, so it's super competitive."

"That sounds awesome, Ag," Cordelia said. "When do you apply?"

"I did," she said with a downcast look.

"They didn't let you in?" Benji asked, mortified on her behalf. "These people are clearly not as smart as you think they are."

"They actually offered me a spot," Agnes said, unable to meet their eyes. "Full scholarship too. But I had to turn them down. It was every day after school and a ton of extra homework. I couldn't do all that and our ghost stuff too."

Cordelia stared at her, stunned.

"Why didn't you tell me?" she asked. "I'm your best friend. I would've talked you into it!"

"Would you?" Agnes asked. "Or would you have told me that my first responsibility was to the ghosts? I was afraid to take the chance."

Cordelia wanted to defend herself, but she suspected that Agnes was right. She looked down, feeling like a horrible friend.

"I'm sorry," she said.

"No worries," Agnes said, brightening. "I can reapply next year. They said there's a spot waiting for me. Apparently I'm 'special.'"

"I could have told them that," Cordelia said.

"What about you, Cord?" Benji asked. "Once we're a ghost-free school, what's the first thing you're going to do?"

Cordelia thought about it. All she really wanted to do was keep spending time with Benji and Agnes. But she had noticed that neither of their post-haunting scenarios included her, so she felt stupid telling them that.

"Mr. Keene seems cool, so I'll probably join Art Club," she said. "Maybe start painting more."

"Nice," Benji said. He turned toward Agnes. "Any idea when the big day is, by the way? And are we having a party? We should have a party."

"I have to recalibrate the pyramids first," she said, "and check to make sure everything is in peak working condition. There's a lot more power coming through this time, so we have to be careful."

"Can I help?" Cordelia asked.

"Sure!" Agnes exclaimed.

"So how does this work long-term?" Benji asked. "Do we just flick the dehaunter on every so often and clear the ghosts out? Like vacuuming?"

Agnes shook her head. "The next time we turn the dehaunter on, it stays on for good," she said. "It'll always be running in the background. Nothing can stop the ghosts from coming, but the dehaunter can make sure their stay is a short one. Shadow School will be like an airport terminal where ghosts wait around for a few hours until they're sent to their final destination."

"Jet *Boo!*" Benji exclaimed, and both girls groaned.

"I actually have to talk to Dr. Roqueni before I can even get started," Agnes said. "She made me promise I wouldn't do anything without consulting her first."

"Did you guys think she was acting a little weird the other night?" Cordelia asked.

"She seemed fine to me," Benji said. "What do you mean?"

"I'm not sure," Cordelia said. "She seemed almost disappointed that the dehaunter worked. I know that sounds crazy, but—"

"Hey, guys!" Vivi said, sliding next to Benji. She spun a green-and-white soccer ball in her hands. "Beware the special today. Ms. Hawkins has been binge-watching cooking shows and is trying to get a little creative with her recipes. Apparently, she put peanut butter and chocolate chips in the meat loaf."

"Hi," Cordelia said, forcing a smile. "We were kind of in the middle of—"

"These are adorable," Vivi said, reaching over to touch Cordelia's earrings. "I love mice."

"They're not mice," Cordelia replied, flustered. "They're rats."

"Cool."

"It's not that I like rats. No one likes rats."

"I like rats," Agnes said.

"It's a Chinese zodiac thing," Cordelia continued. "I was born in the Year of the Rat. My nainai bought these for me when I was in San Francisco."

"Nainai?"

"Grandma."

"Nainai," Vivi repeated. "I love the sound of that. It makes me miss my *abuela*, though. She's the only one who ever bought me jewelry." A hint of sadness cracked her smile, but it didn't last for long. "You playing today?" she asked Benji, tossing him the soccer ball. She and Benji often played together behind the school during recess. "Mason's talking smack because we lost yesterday. I figured you'd want revenge."

"That's my goal!" Benji exclaimed. "Get it? Goal?"

Vivi looked at the other two girls and rolled her eyes. Agnes started to laugh, then saw Cordelia's serious expression and cleared her throat instead.

"I thought we were going to the library during recess," Cordelia said. "I still had some things I wanted to talk to you about"—she paused, catching herself before she revealed too much in front of Vivi—"our math homework."

"I wouldn't go to the library," Vivi said. "Francesca said Ms. Mooney's been acting really strange lately. Why don't you play with us instead?"

"Sorry," Cordelia said, glaring at Benji. "I have more important things to do."

She picked up her tray of half-eaten fries and dumped it in the trash can, feeling their eyes on her back. *Why is Vivi sitting at our table?* she thought. *We're supposed to be talking about the ghosts, not stupid soccer games at stupid recess.*

A football smacked into the trash can, nearly hitting her in the arm.

"Seriously?" Cordelia screamed at Mason James as he retrieved the ball. Mason ignored her and whizzed the football across the lunchroom. It skipped along a table—knocking down cartons of chocolate milk like bowling pins—before one of Mason's pals snagged it and broke into an elaborate dance. Looking around the lunchroom, Cordelia saw that they weren't the only ones fooling around. There were a bunch of kids using their cell phones and even a few building a tower out of milk cartons.

Why aren't they getting in trouble? Cordelia thought, scanning the lunchroom. At first, she didn't see any teacher at all, which would have explained it. But then she saw a single woman staring out the large window in the back.

"Mrs. Machen?" she mumbled to herself in disbelief.

Cordelia's math teacher was the last person she would have expected to let the kids misbehave. Whenever she was on lunch duty, even the bad kids kept their conversations to a whisper. Despite her age, Mrs. Machen still had eagle eyes that could catch a student pulling out a phone or chewing gum from a mile away.

Right now, she was ignoring them completely.

"Everything okay, Mrs. Machen?" Cordelia asked.

Mrs. Machen didn't seem to hear her. She was standing so close to the window that her breath misted the glass.

"Mrs. Machen?" Cordelia repeated, taking a step closer. "You're scaring me a little here."

"It's spectacular," Mrs. Machen said.

Cordelia couldn't argue with that. The window offered a breathtaking view of the White Mountains, particularly Mount Washington, which towered over the neighboring peaks. Cordelia preferred Ludlow's pride and joy in the winter, when it was topped with snow, but there was no denying its majesty even now.

"My parents and I drove up to the top last year," Cordelia said. "I couldn't believe how close the car gets to the edge. My mom's hands turned white, she was clenching the steering wheel so hard. Have you been?"

Mrs. Machen shook her head.

"Oh," Cordelia said, surprised. Mrs. Machen had lived in Ludlow her entire life, so Cordelia figured that scaling Mount Washington would be old hat by now. "You should definitely check it out. It's even cooler from the top."

Mrs. Machen slowly turned her head and regarded Cordelia with a crooked smile. "Soon," she said.

13

Blame

Heart pounding, Cordelia ran through a once-magnificent kitchen that had been demoted to storage room, the disgraced island at its center weighted down with moldering boxes of files and textbooks. Only the old dumbwaiter in the back wall remained unchanged. Essentially a tiny elevator for objects instead of people, it had once been used to transport trays of food to the dining room directly above them.

Like so many things in Shadow School, the dumbwaiter had a secret.

Cordelia pulled its rolling door halfway closed three times in a row, and then all the way down once. When she opened the door again, the back wall had slid out of view, revealing an entrance into darkness. After clicking her trusty flashlight to life, Cordelia squeezed through the hole and joined the narrow pyramid passageway that started in the boiler room. She hurried upward, the sloped floor winding like the stairs of a tower, until she reached the wooden walkway that scraped the bottom of the roof. Even with the flashlight, it was difficult to see. A few work lights hung from the thick wire that ran from pyramid to pyramid, but they were like fireflies against the windowless dark.

"Sorry I'm late!" she exclaimed, seeing Benji and Agnes. "I meant to come here straightaway, but . . ."

"You freed a few ghosts first," Benji said. "We figured."

"How'd it go?" Agnes asked.

"Zero for three," Cordelia said. "Right Brightkeys, no takers."

"Agnes was just explaining how all this works," Benji said, shining his flashlight across the strange latticework that lined the inside of the walls. "Basically, these webs are like solar panels. Only instead of soaking up energy from the sun, they soak up energy from the ghosts."

"Check this out," Agnes said.

She twisted one of the triangles, and a circle of purplish light spread across the wall. It reminded Cordelia of a field trip she had once taken to a cavern known for its luminescent minerals.

"Pretty," she said.

"The same thing happens in the other passageway," Agnes said. "Only the light there isn't purple—it's kind of this lime green. I'm not sure why it's different."

Agnes twisted the triangle back to its original position, and the light vanished. She then ran her fingers along a thin copper wire that connected the wall to a thicker wire running over their heads. "That energy passes along here and gathers in one of the black pyramids, which sends it down to the dehaunter. Our job today is to make sure that each of these thin wires is properly connected. They fall off easily."

Agnes demonstrated on a dangling wire behind Cordelia, pinching it between two fingers, then kneeling down to pull it closer to the web. "Can I get some light, please?" she asked, and Cordelia shone her flashlight over the place where Agnes was working. Slowly and methodically, she threaded the wire through a tiny metal bracket and pulled it taut.

Benji spun around, raising his flashlight so it illuminated the walls behind them.

"What is it?" Cordelia asked.

"Thought I saw something," he said. "Probably nothing."

They continued along the narrow passageway, checking each wire carefully, until they reached one of the black pyramids. There was a neon-green sticky note stuck to its surface with *Banquo* written in black Sharpie.

"Banquo?" Benji asked.

"I named the pyramids after famous ghosts so I could keep them straight," Agnes said with a slight flush of embarrassment. "Banquo is from *Macbeth*. Marley and Zero are right around the bend. The other passageway has my favorites, though. Blinky, Pinky, Inky, and Clyde!"

Benji and Cordelia stared at her blankly.

"Those are the ghosts in *Pac-Man*!" Agnes exclaimed. She shook her head. "I'm disappointed in both of you."

They got back to work. It wasn't the most exciting job in the world, but Cordelia didn't mind. Nothing seemed boring when she was with her friends. As they neared the end of the first passageway, however, Cordelia began to grow worried. *When the ghosts are gone, will we keep doing things together like this? It's not like we're that similar. Benji's a jock. Agnes is a genius. And I'm just . . . me. What if the ghosts are the glue that holds our friendship together?*

"I'm kind of zonked," Cordelia said as they walked toward the supply closet that led to the second set of pyramids. "Why don't we finish this tomorrow? Or next week, even."

Cordelia knew that they would use the dehaunter eventually. She just wanted to keep things the way they were for a little while longer.

"I'm not leaving until we're done," Benji said with the determined look he usually reserved for soccer tournaments. "But no worries if you're bushed. We can finish up without you."

"Besides, Dr. Roqueni said I should drop by her apartment before I go home," Agnes said, "and I'd really like to tell her we're ready to go. This way we can start freeing the ghosts tomorrow if we want!"

Cordelia stopped in her tracks. "Tomorrow?"

"Isn't that a good thing?" Agnes asked.

"It's kind of fast."

"The faster the better," Benji said.

Cordelia looked back and forth between Benji and Agnes, wondering how they could be so excited about the dehaunter despite all the strange things that had been happening. *Is it me?* she wondered. *Am I just making things up in my head because I'm worried that my friends won't want to hang out with me after the ghosts are gone?* She thought about it for a moment and decided there was more to it than that. Something about the entire situation felt off to her—and it had nothing to do with their friendship whatsoever.

"I think we should wait," she said.

"Why?" Benji asked, scoffing.

"Because if there's one thing Shadow School has taught me, it's that you shouldn't mess with things you don't understand. And right now, there're a ton of things I don't understand. Why are more and more ghosts refusing their Brightkeys?"

Benji slapped his forehead. "This again."

"Where are they going afterward? Can they all just leave their ghost zones and roam around the school like the gardener? And another thing." She turned toward Benji. "Maybe you haven't noticed because you've been so distracted, but some of the teachers have been acting kinda weird. There's the headaches, and the whole Mrs. Machen staring out the window thing, and Dr. Roqueni—"

"How have I been 'distracted'?" Benji asked. "Are you talking about Vivi?"

"I meant the dehaunter," Cordelia said, hands on hips. "But now that you mention it—"

"She's not a distraction," Benji said. "She's my friend. Am I not allowed to have friends now?"

"Of course you're allowed to have friends!" Cordelia exclaimed, feeling her insides start to boil. "And don't worry, once you get rid of the ghosts you can spend lots of time with her! I know that's why you want to dehaunt the school so badly!"

"Are you for real?" Benji asked.

"We're not getting rid of the ghosts," Agnes said. "We're freeing them. That's a big difference. Sometimes you forget that Benji and I want to help them as much as you do."

"Please," Cordelia said. "You just want them to go away so you can go to your smart-kid class." She spun on Benji and jabbed a finger in his chest. "And you just want to play all-star soccer so you can impress your new girlfriend. Everything was *perfect*. And now it's all falling apart. I wish we'd never found that stupid machine!"

She ran off, leaving her friends in stunned silence.

That night, Cordelia tossed and turned in bed, wishing she could rewind eight hours and undo her harsh words. It had been unfair to claim that Benji and Agnes didn't want to help the ghosts. They had proven otherwise time and time again. Besides, after hours of thought, she had finally figured out the real reason she was so worried about attending a Shadow School without ghosts.

Back in San Francisco, Cordelia had been one of the most popular girls in school. She wore the right clothes, hung out with the right kids, said the right things. Everyone wanted to be her friend. Then she moved to Ludlow and found out that she was someone else entirely. It was more than just being able to see the ghosts. She had discovered that she could be brave and selfless. Maybe even a little heroic.

She liked this new Cordelia a lot better.

Now that they were on the verge of dehaunting the school, she should have been thrilled—but all she could think about was how different her life would become afterward. What if she went back to being the self-absorbed old Cordelia? Agnes and Benji wouldn't want to stay friends with someone like that. She wouldn't want to *be* someone like that.

Stop thinking about yourself, Cordelia thought as the morning sun began to slant across her bedroom floor. *The important thing is to rescue the ghosts, and the best way to do that is with the dehaunter. If the teachers are still acting weird afterward, we'll figure it out. And if Agnes and Benji don't want to stay friends with me? I'll be really sad—but at least the ghosts will be free. That's the most important thing.*

After the bus brought her to school, Cordelia waited by the front gate, eager to tell her friends about her change of heart. Agnes's bus pulled up shortly afterward—but she didn't get off. Benji wasn't on his bus, either.

Weird, Cordelia thought.

She supposed that they could have come to school early to do some final checks on the dehaunter—especially if Dr. Roqueni had decided that today was going to be the big day. Cordelia felt a little hurt that they hadn't included her, but after last night, could she really blame them?

It was only when Cordelia didn't see them at the lockers that she started to feel the first inklings of trepidation. *Where are they?* Then, at last, she saw Agnes heading in her direction. Judging by her lank hair and hollowed-out eyes, her best friend's night had been no more restful than her own.

"There you are," Cordelia said with a big smile. She had planned out a whole dramatic speech during the bus ride to school. Now that the moment was upon her, however, Cordelia couldn't remember a single word. She decided to start with the simplest, most powerful phrase of all.

"I'm sorry," she said.

Agnes squeezed her eyes shut and set loose twin rivulets of tears.

"How could you?" she screamed, clenching her hands into fists. "You ruined everything! *Everything!*"

Cordelia stared at her in bewilderment.

"Agnes?" she asked as a crowd began to gather around them. Cordelia saw a bunch of students filming her with their cell phones. "I don't know what you're—"

"You just couldn't bear the thought of me being the hero for once!" Agnes exclaimed, jabbing a finger at Cordelia's chest. "*You* have to be their savior, or it doesn't count. That's the real reason you destroyed it. *You!*"

Cordelia shook her head. The hallway wobbled beneath her feet.

"I have no idea what you're talking about."

"You're nothing but a big fat liar," Agnes said, bending over with her hands on her thighs. It was as though her uncharacteristic display of anger had drained all her energy.

"Agnes," Cordelia said, reaching out for her friend. "Just tell me what's going on. Please."

Agnes slapped her hand away and vanished into the crowd. Cordelia started after her, tears blurring her vision, but Benji cut through the students and blocked her path.

"Let her go," he said.

"Benji!" Cordelia exclaimed, grabbing his arm. "She thinks I did something, but I have no idea what she's talking about."

Benji refused to meet her eyes.

"Don't deny it, Cordelia. I saw what you did."

He left before she could ask him a single question. *Not him too*, Cordelia thought, backing away until she felt her locker against her back. *What's happening? Why are they both so mad at me?*

As the crowd began to disperse, Cordelia saw Dr. Roqueni talking to Benji and Agnes at the end of the hall. The principal nodded and squeezed Agnes's shoulder, then approached Cordelia. Her back was straight, her lips taut.

"Please tell me what's going on," Cordelia whispered.

Dr. Roqueni leaned forward so that only Cordelia could hear her words.

"I am so amazingly disappointed in you. I think it would be best if you stayed away from us from now on. Don't go to Elijah's office. Don't talk to Benji or Agnes. Go straight home after school. As of now, you're just a normal student. Got it?"

"Dr. Roqueni?" Cordelia asked, but the principal had already started to walk away. Benji and Agnes followed her. Cordelia tried to call after them, but it took a few tries before she could force words past the violent sobs racking her body.

"Will someone please tell me what's going on?"

Benji turned around. Unlike Agnes, he didn't look angry. He looked sad.

"You made a choice, Cordelia," he said. "You could have kept your friends or the ghosts. You chose the ghosts."

He slipped his arm around Agnes's shoulders and led her away.

When Cordelia had finally gathered her senses, she realized the only possible meaning of Agnes's words—*That's the real reason you destroyed it!*—and hurried down the long ladder to the dehaunter. It was nothing more than a mound of dust and splinters. A black sledgehammer leaned haughtily against the wall, looking satisfied by a job well done.

Mr. Derleth was sweeping the debris into a black trash bag. He had already accumulated five of them, lined up against the wall. When he caught sight of Cordelia, he stopped sweeping and glared at her.

"Come to revisit the scene of the crime?" he asked.

"It wasn't me," Cordelia said with a hint of anger. She was growing tired of being blamed for something she didn't do.

Mr. Derleth scoffed and went back to sweeping.

"'I wish we'd never found that stupid machine,'" he

said. "Your words. Agnes told us all about it."

"I was mad. I didn't actually mean it."

"You expect me to believe that?"

"Actually, yes," Cordelia said. "You know me, Mr. Derleth. I do a lot of stupid things. But I'm not, like, a bad person. I would never destroy something that could help the ghosts."

"Who did it, then?" he asked, tying the bag in a tight knot and adding it to the others. "Me? Dr. Roqueni? Benji or Agnes? We're the only five who know this room even exists. And of the five of us, who's the one who never seemed sold on the idea of dehaunting the school?"

"Because I think there's something weird going on," Cordelia said. "And this only proves my point! First the ghosts start refusing their Brightkeys. Then someone destroys a machine that's basically one giant Bright-key. Do you think that's a coincidence? I sure don't. Someone—or something—doesn't want the ghosts to go into their Brights."

For just a moment, she saw a flicker of astonishment in Mr. Derleth's eyes, as though Cordelia had hit upon a truth he'd never expected her to find. He looked away, but it was too late.

"Do you know something about this, Mr. Derleth?" she asked.

He scowled and took a step in her direction, before seeming to catch himself. Cordelia shuddered. For a moment, she had glimpsed something unsettling in Mr. Derleth's usually gentle features. Something she had never seen before.

"The only thing I know," Mr. Derleth said, his voice soft and measured, "is that you're the one who destroyed the dehaunter. Now get out of here and let me finish cleaning up your mess."

Cordelia hurried back up the ladder. Behind her, she heard the *swish swish* of the broom.

14

Experiment

Bulletin boards, a school's true calendar, had shed their orange skin in favor of football brown. A parade of thankful essays marched in five-part harmony. Occasionally a breeze—or something more than a breeze—fluttered the pages.

Cordelia trudged past the displays without really seeing them. She wasn't feeling particularly thankful. Although she had tried to explain herself on multiple occasions, Benji and Agnes still refused to talk to her. Eventually, she had given up. Benji seemed happy enough hanging out with Vivi and his soccer buddies, but she was worried about Agnes. Dr. Roqueni had given her permission to skip all her classes so she could work on an "enrichment project" all day long. After days of searching, Cordelia had finally found Agnes tucked away in a tiny classroom, hunched over a table covered with blueprints. Mr. Derleth sat with his feet on the desk, watching her work.

She must be building a new dehaunter, Cordelia thought, ducking beneath the window so Mr. Derleth wouldn't see her. After their last encounter, she had avoided him altogether. Although she wanted to trust him, Cordelia couldn't shake the suspicion that he knew more about the entire situation than he was letting on.

Could he have been the one who destroyed the dehaunter? she wondered. *But that doesn't make any sense. He's our friend! And why would he be helping Agnes build a new one, then?*

Cordelia figured that if she kept tabs on Agnes's progress, she might uncover some answers. But when she came back the next day, the window in the class-room door had been covered with black paper.

It was the first day back from Thanksgiving break. Ms. Jackson was standing at the door, greeting the students, as Cordelia entered room 313. The science teacher hadn't fled the classroom in several weeks, and while she still wrung her hands whenever a student asked a question, her mumbling had been limited to the occasional "You can do this!"

There was a lab that day, and Ms. Jackson assigned each student to a specific table. Cordelia found herself sitting with the unlikely trio of Mason James, a studious boy named Henry Gull, and Vivi.

Ugh, she thought, tossing her bookbag on the floor. *Just when I thought things couldn't get any worse.*

"Hey, Cordelia," Vivi said. "How was your Thanksgiving?"

"Fine. Yours?"

"Nice. Benji and his family came for dessert. His sisters are so cute. Have you met them?"

"Lots of times. They're sweet. Well, maybe not Sofia. She's a little much."

"Totally. She kept asking if Benji and I were 'regular friends' or 'kissy friends.'"

Well, which one is it? Cordelia almost asked, but Mason inserted himself into the conversation and started bragging about his family's lake house in Maine. It was clear how badly he wanted to impress Vivi, who smiled politely while searching her backpack for a pen.

Not gonna happen, Mason, Cordelia thought. *She's into Benji, not you.*

At least the lab was kind of fun. After reading the directions to the class, Ms. Jackson gave each table a tray of eight Dixie cups filled with different liquids

(Cordelia recognized most of them, such as vinegar and milk, but an orange, viscous fluid remained a mystery). Their assignment was to use pH strips and a special chart to determine each liquid's level of acidity. To Cordelia's surprise, her group worked well together. She and Vivi dipped the strips into the liquid and tried to match the resultant color to the chart, while Henry recorded the answers on their lab report. At some point, Mason—who wasn't actually doing anything—wandered off to the windows that looked upon the adjacent classrooms. There were two classes in progress, and he was having a great time smooshing his butt against the glass every time Mr. Langan or Ms. Straub turned around.

"My friends all say Mason is cute," Vivi said, "but I think he's kind of a jerk."

"Kind of?" Cordelia asked. "He's literally the worst person I know. And that's including my uncle Phil, who smells like damp towels and always pretends he forgot his wallet when we go out to dinner."

Vivi laughed. "You're funny."

"People keep telling me that."

Cordelia noticed Benji watching them. When he saw that Cordelia was looking in his direction, he spun around on his stool.

"He's such an idiot," Vivi said.

"Mason?"

"Benji," she said. "I don't know why you two are fighting, but I've seen you try to talk to him. He's not even giving you a chance. What's he thinking? You guys were inseparable. You don't just throw that away!"

For a few moments, Cordelia was too surprised to speak. She had assumed that Vivi would be thrilled that she and Benji were no longer on speaking terms. The last thing she had expected was for Vivi to take her side.

"He thinks I did something bad," Cordelia said. "Only I didn't actually do it."

"Did you tell him that?"

"Many, many times."

"He'll come around," Vivi said. "If you want, I can help you. I'll ask him to meet me after school, only it will be you instead, and we'll lock the door until everything is fixed."

"You'd do that?" Cordelia asked.

"Sure! He misses you. You were all he could talk about when we went sledding yesterday."

Cordelia was immediately blindsided by an image that made her stomach hurt. *Benji and Vivi on a sled together, falling, laughing* . . .

"Thanks for offering," Cordelia said. "But this is between me and Benji. You don't need to get involved."

Vivi looked hurt. "I was just trying to help."

"Hello," Henry said, waving his hand back and forth. "This is totally fascinating, but could we please get back to work now?"

Vivi nodded and bent across the table for the next Dixie cup. Over her back, Cordelia saw the ghost that had just entered the room. It was an old woman wearing a pink robe, her swollen ankles mapped with angry veins. Her grin was toothless, her gray hair wet and glistening. Drops of water fell to the floor and vanished.

Her Brightkey is a shower cap, Cordelia remembered. *I offered it to her weeks ago. She refused.*

"This one's close, but I think it's acidic, right?" Vivi asked, all business now as she tried to match the pH strip—which had turned light green—to the chart. Cordelia nodded while keeping tabs on the ghost, who was shuffling between the tables on slippered feet and examining each student. She stopped to take a particularly long look at Miranda before continuing her tour.

This one's out of her ghost zone, just like the gardener, Cordelia thought. *But what exactly is she doing? Looking for someone?*

Cordelia glanced in Benji's direction, hoping that he was seeing this, but his back was still turned. Before she could whisper his name, the ghost headed toward her table.

Just ignore her, Cordelia thought, facing forward. *She'll leave soon.*

Cordelia retrieved the last Dixie cup from the tray and held it still while Vivi lowered the strip of pH paper into the orange liquid. From the corner of her eye, Cordelia saw the old woman staring down at them. She dismissed Cordelia with a passing glance and bent down to examine Vivi more closely.

"It's chunky," Vivi said, scrunching her nose with disgust as she lifted the pH strip. Watching carefully, the old woman imitated the expression. Vivi pushed a strand of hair back over one ear. The old woman did the same.

What's that all about? Cordelia thought. *Ghosts usually ignore the living. Not imitate them.*

"You okay?" Vivi asked, waving a hand in front of Cordelia's eyes. "Is this about what I said before? I'm sorry if I stuck my nose where it doesn't belong."

The old woman was still staring at Vivi. Her eyes had grown wide and hungry.

Cordelia felt the back of her neck prickle. *Something isn't right here,* she thought.

The ghost clenched her eyes shut, blew out her cheeks like a stubborn child attempting to hold her breath for as long as possible, and placed her hands on

Vivi's shoulders. Cordelia expected Vivi to wince with pain at being touched by a ghost, but she showed no reaction whatsoever.

"I know things might be a little weird right now," Vivi said, giving Cordelia a smile as the ghost's face turned red with strain. "But I really hope that we can be friends."

"Totally," Cordelia murmured, barely listening. The ghost had begun to fade away. Her now-transparent fingers tightened their grip on Vivi's shoulders.

"Is everything okay?" Vivi asked. "You look pale."

The old woman was practically gone now.

Vivi winced and rubbed her temples. "Ow," she said.

While Cordelia's mind scrambled to work out what was happening, her instincts screamed at her to get the old woman away from Vivi as quickly as possible. Without thinking, she grabbed the nearest Dixie cup and flung its contents at Vivi's chest. Orange fluid splattered everywhere. Vivi screamed and jumped off her stool, causing the barely visible ghost to lose her grip. She immediately reappeared and snarled at Cordelia, furious at the interruption.

"You're crazy!" Vivi exclaimed, more baffled than angry. Orange, chunky liquid ran down the front of her white shirt. "No wonder Benji doesn't like you anymore!"

She ran out of the room.

"Get out of here," Ms. Jackson said, her voice firmer than Cordelia had ever heard it before. "Right now."

Cordelia took a step toward the door before she realized that the teacher's words had not been intended for her.

They were meant for the ghost.

There was no doubt about it. Ms. Jackson was looking directly at the old woman. *She has the Sight*, Cordelia thought, mouth agape. Even stranger, the ghost seemed *scared* of the timid teacher. She lowered her head like a wounded dog and began backing away.

Ms. Jackson turned her attention toward Cordelia.

"Sorry," Cordelia mumbled, raising the Dixie cup in her hand. "It slipped."

She saw Benji throw his hands into the air: *What is wrong with you?* Everyone—even the students in the adjoining classrooms—was staring at her.

Except for Mr. Langan. Like Ms. Jackson, he was looking straight at the ghost.

He can see her too? Cordelia thought, her mind reeling.

Ms. Jackson cleared her throat. "Recess detention," she said. "Three days."

Cordelia nodded meekly. She thought it was telling that Ms. Jackson didn't ask her why she'd done it. *Why bother?* Cordelia thought. *She saw the ghost. She knows my reason.*

The class returned to relative normalcy. Benji refused to look in her direction. Mason gave Cordelia a nod of approval, as though she had just gained entrance into some club she had never wanted to be a part of.

At least the ghost is gone, Cordelia thought. Through the windows, she could see the old woman shuffle down the hallway. Ms. Straub, who taught health next door, stepped out of her classroom.

The ghost glanced in her direction. Ms. Straub waved her along.

"She can see ghosts too?" Cordelia mumbled under her breath. "You gotta be kidding me!"

Henry gave her a nervous look and slid the tray of samples beyond her reach.

15

Proof

By the end of the week, Cordelia had identified three more teachers who could see the ghosts.

It was hard to miss the signs once you knew to look for them. Mr. Hearn sidestepped a skateboarding spirit so smoothly that he didn't even spill his coffee. Mrs. LaValle winked at a dead cowboy. Mrs. Machen stared daggers at any ghost that came within ten feet of her until they went away. It was basically the same way she treated the children.

Cordelia found the fact that her math teacher had the Sight of particular interest. For one thing, she was positive that Mrs. Machen had been unable to see the ghosts last year. She also remembered that bizarre afternoon in the lunchroom when Mrs. Machen had pressed her fingers against the window and looked longingly at the view of Mount Washington. It was odd behavior for a woman who had lived her entire life in Ludlow.

And then, of course, there was what had happened to Vivi—the way the ghost vanished as it touched her and seemed to give Vivi a headache, just like the teachers.

It has to be connected, Cordelia thought.

A theory was beginning to develop in her head. It didn't answer everything—not by a long shot—but it answered *some* things. Cordelia knew exactly where she needed to go to find out whether she was right, but there was one major problem: If she went alone, any discovery she made would be useless since Benji and Agnes didn't trust her anymore. She wanted—needed—them to believe her, and right now that would only happen if they witnessed it with their own eyes. It didn't have to be both of them. Agnes and Benji still trusted each other, so as long as she had one of them to back up her story, everything would be fine.

So which one should she bring?

Agnes would have been her first choice, but there was no way for Cordelia to get her alone and state her case; she spent all day in her little classroom and hardly ever came out. Even when she did, Mr. Derleth was always by her side. She seemed more like a prisoner than a student.

It would have to be Benji.

Now all Cordelia had to do was convince him to help her.

They were playing basketball in gym that day. Last year, Mr. Bruce had always made them stretch and do a few warm-up activities first, then assigned them to teams based on their skill level. He had been far more lax this year. Today, for instance, he just nodded to the ball rack and told them to figure it out. When Cordelia complained of a sore ankle, he shrugged and sent her to the bleachers.

He hasn't been acting like himself, Cordelia thought. *Just like Dr. Roqueni and Mr. Derleth.*

Hopefully that meant she had chosen the right teacher for her demonstration.

Benji was lazing on the bleachers with a group of his soccer buddies, including Vivi. To their right, Mason and his crew were making fun of a boy trying to shoot a foul shot.

As soon as Mason saw Cordelia, he redirected his sneer toward her. "Watch out, fellas," he said. "Here comes crazy."

Cordelia ignored him and headed straight for Benji's group. Vivi regarded Cordelia with a cautious look, as though there might be a Dixie cup filled with mango juice hidden behind her back.

"I'm sorry about the other day," Cordelia said. "I wish I could explain, but you wouldn't believe me."

She stooped down over Benji.

"Run, Núñez! She's going in for a kiss!" Mason shouted, sending his minions into spasms of snorting, ugly laughter.

"Get lost, Cordelia," Benji said, turning away. "I don't want to talk to you."

"Watch Mr. Bruce," she whispered in his ear.

Ignoring the hoots and insults being leveled at her, Cordelia took a seat on the top row of the bleachers. There was another boy sitting there. He looked like he would have been in high school, had he lived. Half his head was shaved clean. The rest of his hair hung over his eyes. His fingernails were painted black.

There was a sketchbook in his lap, open to a blank page.

"Cool pad," Cordelia said, rummaging through her backpack. "I'm an artist, too."

She pulled out her fancy set of graphite pencils and selected a freshly sharpened 4B. The boy looked like he might favor darker lines.

"Try this one," she said, placing the pencil on the bench next to him.

The ghost gave her an aloof nod—as though she had

done nothing more than let him borrow a pencil for a math test—and took the Brightkey. A triangle opened high above them. At first Cordelia saw only blue sky, but as she slid along the bleachers and angled her view, she was able to glimpse the Eiffel Tower in the distance.

The boy began to rise.

"What are you doing?" Benji asked, rushing up the bleachers. "Someone will see!"

He had a point: sometimes a triangle's appearance produced an inexplicable breeze or screwed with nearby electrical devices. Fortunately, this Bright seemed as chill as its owner. Cordelia could smell freshly baked baguettes and hear the *ding-ding* of a bicycle bell, but that was just because she had the Sight. There was the small matter of the pencil, which would appear to be rising on its own, but everyone was too caught up in their games to notice.

Almost everyone.

"Watch Mr. Bruce," Cordelia whispered to Benji. "Just don't look like you're watching him."

Benji rolled his eyes but did as she asked. Cordelia remained focused on the ghost, who dropped his Brightkey—as she suspected he might—and descended to the floor. He paused to give Cordelia an apologetic shrug and floated toward the door of the gym. As the ghost passed Mr. Bruce, the gym teacher gave him a victorious fist pump, as though he had just kicked the winning goal in a championship game.

Cordelia saw Benji's mouth drop open. She smiled.

Mr. Bruce can see the ghosts, she thought. *And now Benji knows it.* She even had a theory as to why Mr. Bruce was so happy that the ghost had refused its Bright. A scary, crazy theory that she hoped wasn't true. But a theory nonetheless.

Benji joined her at the top of the bleachers. "Mr. Bruce has the Sight," he said, his voice a little shaky. "That's what you wanted me to see, isn't it?"

Cordelia nodded.

"How long have you known?"

"About Mr. Bruce? I didn't. Not for sure. Until just now, I mean."

Benji scratched his forehead. "Then how did you know I should watch him?"

"Because Mr. Bruce isn't the only teacher who can see the ghosts. I've confirmed six other ones. I'm guessing there'll be more."

"That's impossible. The Sight is super rare."

"You're right," Cordelia said. "That's why I don't think it's the Sight."

"Hey, Núñez!" Mason called out. "We're gonna show those losers over there how to play basketball. You in?"

"Later," Benji said.

"Whatever," Mason said. He stomped past Vivi, who paused to give Benji and Cordelia a confused look before heading over to join a game of her own.

"What do you mean it's not the Sight?" Benji asked, taking a seat next to Cordelia. "If these teachers can see ghosts, what else can it be?"

"I have a theory," Cordelia said. "Just promise me you'll keep an open mind."

"Sure. I mean, at this point, how can things get any weirder?"

Cordelia laughed. "Hold on to that thought," she said. "So, what if it's not really the teachers who are seeing the ghosts? What if it's something *inside* the teachers?"

"Huh?"

"People can't see ghosts. Not without the Sight. But ghosts can see other ghosts just fine."

"Ghosts can see other ghosts . . ." Benji muttered, turning the words over in his head. "Are you telling me that these teachers are *dead*?"

"No," Cordelia said. "Don't be ridiculous. They're just possessed."

"Possessed?" Benji asked, rubbing the back of his neck. "For real?"

"Open mind! You promised!"

"Mind wide open," he reassured her. "But we've never seen the ghosts possess anyone before. That's not their thing."

"Not usually," Cordelia said, folding her hands on her lap. "Most cases of possession involve demons or other entities. But it's not unheard of. I read about a few examples online. It would explain how these teachers are able to see the ghosts. And why they've been acting so strange. And the headaches! I mean, if a ghost takes control of your brain, it's bound to make your head hurt!"

"Obviously," Benji said, still not buying it.

"Plus, there's what happened with Vivi," Cordelia said.

Benji leaned forward.

"What does she have to do with it?"

"There was a ghost in science. An old woman. She touched Vivi, and then she started to disappear. I think she was going into Vivi's body. That's why I threw the mango juice. I was trying to stop her."

Benji rubbed his temples with both hands, and Cordelia felt a cold rush of panic.

Oh no, she thought. *What if he's—*

"I'm not possessed," he said, noticing her frightened expression. "This is just a lot."

"I know."

"Vivi said you threw the juice at her because you're jealous."

Cordelia's face grew warm. She took a deep breath before replying. "That's ridiculous. I was trying to scare off the ghost. Vivi would know that if she could see them."

Benji nodded and played with the strings of his hoodie. "That makes sense, I guess. Why would you be jealous? It's not like . . . you know?"

"Exactly."

"But how come I didn't see this ghost?" Benji asked. "I was right there."

"Your back was turned."

Benji looked down at his lap. "That's kind of convenient," he said.

"What's that supposed to mean? You think I'm making this up?"

"I don't know!" Benji exclaimed. "I want to believe you. Actually, I don't want to believe you, because this entire possession thing sounds terrifying, but . . . I want to trust you. Like I used to."

"Then do it!"

"How can I after what you did to the dehaunter?"

"For the last time," Cordelia said, "I did not touch that stupid thing! Why doesn't anyone believe me?"

"Because Agnes saw you do it," Benji said.

Cordelia's mouth fell open. "What?"

"Agnes went down to the dehaunter to make some final adjustments, and she saw you smashing it to pieces. She told us everything."

"*Agnes* said that?"

"Yeah."

"Agnes Matheson?"

"Why are you so surprised? You were there. You know what you did."

Cordelia shook her head. "She lied to you."

"No way," Benji said. "She could barely tell us what happened because she was crying so hard. Unless Agnes has a side gig as an Academy Award–winning actress, she had to be telling the truth."

"But she's not, Benji. I'd kinda know."

Cordelia chewed her lower lip, befuddled. *Could Agnes have seen someone else who looked like me? Could I have an evil double?*

That seemed a stretch, even for Shadow School.

"Why would Agnes lie?" Benji asked.

"I don't know," Cordelia said. "I'd ask her, but she doesn't talk to me anymore."

"She doesn't talk to me much, either," Benji said. "She spends all her time in this one classroom, working on a new dehaunter." He threw his head back in disgust. "This is all so confusing, but you're definitely right about one thing. Something weird is going on."

"So help me figure it out," Cordelia said. "Let's start with all these faculty meetings. What are those all about?"

Benji shrugged. "Just boring teacher stuff."

"I don't think so," Cordelia said. "It's crazy how much they meet. And haven't you noticed that all this weirdness started about the same time as the meetings? We need to know what they're up to."

"But how?" Benji asked. "It's not like we can just sneak into a"—he sighed, realization setting in—"Oh, man. That's exactly what you want to do, isn't it?"

"Pretty much."

"I don't know," Benji said, rising to his feet. "I need to think about this."

Cordelia grabbed his hand, holding him there a little longer.

"After all we've been through, don't you think I've earned a little trust?"

"I've gotta go," Benji said. He ran down the bleachers without turning around once.

Cordelia saw Mr. Bruce watching him with a suspicious expression on his face. His eyes flicked toward Cordelia.

She looked away.

16

Faculty Meeting

Three days later, Cordelia received a text from Benji.

I'm in, he wrote.

Cordelia queued up a line of smiley-face emojis before deciding it was too much. She erased them and responded with a simple Cool.

I'm not saying I believe you, Benji texted. But I don't not believe you.

Good enough. For now.

I went to see A today. In that room. To tell her all this.

What did she say?

That's the thing. Mr. D wouldn't let me talk to her. He actually yelled at me for even trying. Mr. D never yelled at me b4.

It's not him, Cordelia texted.

I think ur right. But then who is it? Why are the ghosts doing this?

Let's find out.

If faculty meetings had still been held in the library, like the previous year, Cordelia and Benji could have simply gotten there early and found a good hiding spot. But Dr. Roqueni had moved meetings to the conservatory, which she had redone over the summer for this express purpose.

The door to the conservatory was always locked.

Stealing the key would be nearly impossible; as far as Cordelia knew, the only copy was on Dr. Roqueni's keychain, which she kept in her pocket at all times. Before even considering such a risky option, Cordelia and Benji decided to do a thorough examination of the nearby rooms, just in case there was a secret door or passageway. Since they didn't want the teachers to know they were planning something, they took turns searching so there was no risk of them being seen together.

It was Benji who struck gold.

Found it! he texted her after school one day. Trapdoor. Mr. Terpin's room.

It goes to the conservatory?

Even better, he replied. It's like a hiding spot. We can see them. They can't see us.

Sounds good! Cordelia wrote. U game tomorrow?

It was a few moments before Benji responded. R we doing something stupid dangerous?????

Of course, Cordelia replied. That's how we roll.

Wish we could ask Agnes. She's smarter than us.

WAY smarter, Cordelia agreed. U could text her . . .

Thought about it. But what if Agnes is acting weird because not Agnes? Possessed??? Can't trust her.

Does that mean u trust me again? Cordelia tried, throwing in a hand emoji with two fingers crossed.

IDK. U could be possessed too.

Cordelia waited for Benji to tell her he was kidding. He never did.

After school the next day, Cordelia met Benji outside Mr. Terpin's classroom. They loitered in the hall while the math teacher wiped down every desk with antibacterial wipes and scrubbed his dry-erase board clean. At last, he flicked off the lights and left. As soon as Mr. Terpin was out of sight, Benji led Cordelia into the room and showed her the trapdoor he had found beneath the teacher's desk. They opened it and hopped down into a large crawl space. Cordelia could stand up—barely— but Benji had to hunch over or his head would graze the ceiling. While Cordelia closed the trapdoor above them, Benji flicked a switch that activated several dusty lights.

"Sweet!" Cordelia said.

The crawl space had the cozy feel of a tree house. There were pillows, a sleeping bag, piles of ancient comic books with titles like *Horrific* and *The Haunt of Fear*, toy cars, and a ton of drawing supplies.

"Who do you think all this stuff belonged to?" Cordelia asked. She made sure to whisper as quietly as possible. The observatory was right below them, and she wasn't sure how far their voices would carry.

Stepping lightly across the floor, Benji led her to a desk constructed from two crates and a piece of plywood. Above this makeshift workspace, dozens of newspaper clippings had been tacked to the wall: "FAMILY ABANDONS HOME DUE TO NIGHTLY 'VISITORS,'" "RETIRED NURSE HEARS VOICE BEHIND WALL, FINDS BODY," "LOCAL MAN CHARGES ADMISSION TO 'HAUNTED' HOUSE." Whoever had pinned the newspaper articles to the wall had also sketched the houses featured in the photographs. The drawings were more technical than artistic, with crisp lines and measurements.

In the right-hand corner of one of the drawings, Cordelia saw a signature. The name was complicated by loops and curlicues—a kid trying to sign his name like a real artist—but after a moment's study, she was able to piece the letters together.

Darius Shadow.

"Guess he lived here at some point before it became a school," Benji said, peeking over her shoulder. "This must have been his special hiding spot."

There were a few other items on the desk: a cigar box filled with eyeglass lenses that had been poked from their frames, a thick accordion folder, tarot cards, and a Magic 8-Ball. Cordelia opened the folder. It was stuffed with more newspaper clippings about ghosts and haunted houses.

"Wow," she said. "Darius really did want to be just like Elijah when he grew up. Which is strange, when you think about it. He couldn't even see the ghosts."

Almost directly beneath their feet, they heard the *click* of a key opening a lock. Benji gasped and pulled Cordelia to the opposite end of the crawl space. The boards squeaking beneath their feet were drowned out by the squealing hinges of the conservatory door.

The teachers were coming.

Benji led her down a five-rung ladder to a cramped area barely big enough for the two of them. He slid a narrow panel to the left and made as much room as possible so she could squeeze next to him. If they had found themselves in the same situation a few weeks ago, Cordelia might have made some kind of joke: *Hope you're wearing deodorant* or *Good thing I'm part elf.* But their friendship hadn't yet knitted itself back together again, so all she could do was smile shyly and hope he didn't mind being so close to her.

They looked through the slot together.

Their vantage point was just below the ceiling, giving them a decent view of the entire conservatory. Although the December sun shining through the arched windows provided little light, the flora seemed to be thriving: a colony of potted plants raised their unruly fronds toward the sky, while ivy twisted around the trellised balcony that encircled the room. A stone fountain covered with moss dribbled brackish water.

Cordelia was so taken with the dark beauty of the conservatory that she didn't see the ghosts at first. There were dozens of them pressed shoulder to shoulder against the windows. Cordelia recognized a teenager wearing a royal-blue prom dress and sparkling tiara. Her Brightkey, a wasted corsage of lavender roses, had been dead and wilted in Cordelia's locker for weeks. It was hard to tell for sure, since none of the ghosts were facing her, but she thought she recognized a few others who had refused their Brightkeys as well.

When she shared this observation with Benji, he nodded his head.

"I see one that turned me down, too," he whispered. "This must be where they've been hiding out since they escaped their ghost zones."

The teachers filed into the room and settled into the chairs set up around the observatory. Cordelia listened closely, hoping to learn something useful, but their conversations were all about normal things like TV shows or their families. When they mentioned the school at all, it was just to complain about someone's annoying parents (such as Mason's mom, who kept accusing the seventh-grade teachers of picking on her "misunderstood angel").

"Nothing's happening," Benji said. "Maybe you got it wrong."

Cordelia saw Mr. Russell take out a bottle of Tylenol and tap a few into his palm.

"Give it more time," she said. "The meeting hasn't even started yet."

A second wave of teachers, led by Dr. Roqueni, entered the conservatory. They didn't speak at all. Mrs. Machen and Mr. Bruce entered last, wheeling a squeaky A/V cart whose odd-shaped cargo was covered by a black sheet. Instead of sitting, the late arrivals spread themselves evenly across the room, like teachers at recess duty. Cordelia was left with the uncomfortable impression that they wanted to make sure no one could leave. Mrs. Aickman, perhaps sensing the same thing, shifted uneasily in her seat.

"Hey, Aria," said Ms. Schwerin, a brash music teacher who seemed completely oblivious to the rising tension in the room. "Can we make this quick? My kid is sick."

"Of course," said Dr. Roqueni. "Let's get right to business."

She raised her hands above her head and clapped them together. "My fellow spirits! Take control of these mortal shells and join me!"

It was as though a switch had been flipped. As one, the teachers began to groan in pain. A few fell forward with their heads clasped in their hands. Others stared straight ahead, backs ramrod straight. Ms. Jackson, showing more tenacity than Cordelia would have ever given her credit for, managed to make it all the way to the door before collapsing to her knees.

A few moments later, the groans stopped. The teachers cracked their necks and stretched their arms, as though they had just awoken from a particularly restful nap.

Ms. Schwerin was the first to speak. "*So* much better," she said.

Mr. Terpin nodded in agreement and took a long, joyous breath. "I never appreciated how sweet the air was when I was alive. But now I can't get enough of it!"

"Hear, hear," agreed Mr. Hearn in a British accent. He tried to applaud, but his hands kept missing each other. "Oh, dear. I had this yesterday."

"Don't force it," Mr. Terpin said. "Remember your lessons—'wear the body like a suit of clothes.'"

Mr. Hearn wasn't the only one having a hard time. Mr. Blender kept sitting and standing for no reason at all. Ms. Soney had gone cross-eyed. Ms. Patel jerked and kicked like a malfunctioning robot. If Cordelia had seen her teachers acting so goofy on any other day, it would have been hilarious.

But this wasn't funny at all.

Cordelia felt Benji's hand slip into her own. It was warm and sweaty and wonderfully real, an anchor that kept her from blowing away into a dark and disobedient world.

"They're possessed," he said, his breathing quick and shallow. "You were right."

"I wish I'd been wrong."

"I don't get it, though. The teachers were normal when they got here. And I didn't see any of the ghosts . . . I don't know . . . hop inside them or anything."

"The ghosts were already inside, waiting," Cordelia whispered. "Dr. Roqueni just woke them up."

Benji shook his head. "That's not Dr. Roqueni," he said.

In a few moments, the ghosts had finished settling into their bodies. They sat up in their seats and gave the principal their full attention. To the uninformed observer, it would have looked like an ordinary faculty meeting.

"Welcome back to the land of the living," she said. "I know how hard it is to keep yourselves buried deep each day and not take control. But you should take pride in how good you've gotten at being passengers! Remember just a few months ago? Most of you couldn't remain in a living body for a few *minutes* without losing your grip!" There were some embarrassed chuckles from the audience. "Now you're able to hide in these breathers from the moment they enter the school in the morning to the moment they go home at night. I'm so proud of you. Show of hands—how many of your hosts don't even get headaches anymore?"

A dozen arms shot into the air. Dr. Roqueni nodded with admiration.

"Wonderful," she said. "Keep practicing, and before long you'll be permitted to take full control during the school day, just like my best students here." She gestured toward the standing teachers, including Mr.

Derleth, Mrs. Machen, and Mr. Bruce. "They've managed to imitate their hosts so perfectly that the little urchins don't know the difference! Work hard and follow their example."

"Yes, Ms. Dunsworth," the teachers intoned.

Benji nudged Cordelia with his shoulder.

"Dunsworth," he said. "That must be the ghost inside Dr. Roqueni."

Cordelia nodded, etching the name into her memory so she could research it later.

"We'll be breaking into groups today," Dr. Roqueni/ Ms. Dunsworth continued. She glanced over at the ghosts standing by the windows. "Those of you who recently refused the temptation of your Brights and joined us"—she paused to lead the other ghosts in a round of applause—"will head down to the fifth-grade classrooms. Julia will teach you the basics of how to squeeze your spirit into a human host, but don't expect to get it the first day. It takes practice."

The teachers nodded in agreement. Ms. Patel offered the ghosts an encouraging thumbs-up.

"One word of warning to our newcomers, however," Ms. Dunsworth said, crossing the room to address the window ghosts directly. "Just because you *can* possess a human doesn't mean you should. If you prove yourself, you will be assigned a shell. By me and me alone.

Do *not* practice your newfound skills without permission." Ms. Dunsworth turned to face the teachers. "And despite the temptation, no one, under any circumstances, should attempt to possess one of the students. Wearing a child is far more difficult than wearing an adult. Their minds and bodies are still developing. That makes them . . . slippery. So much can go wrong—and we can't risk being revealed."

The teachers nodded. It was clearly not the first time they had heard this warning.

"Some of you may decide to risk it anyway. You may think, 'That Ms. Dunsworth is a hundred and fifty years old. I'm sure I can get away with it!' If that happens, please remember dear Martha. Such an amusing spirit, in her bathrobe and slippers. Until she lost her head and tried to possess a child—in front of a girl with the Sight, no less! I can't allow that. I *won't* allow that—as Martha learned."

Cordelia saw a few teachers glance back at the A/V cart. She had no idea what lay beneath its black sheet, but based on their fearful expressions, she suspected it had something to do with Martha's punishment.

Ms. Dunsworth left the ghosts by the windows and returned to her original position in front of the teachers. She pulled a Post-it note from her pocket and glanced down at it.

169

"Let's see . . . if you're fumbling over words—'dead mouth,' as we call it—please work with Jane today. She's prepared a few special tongue twisters for you to loosen up those muscles. There will be a fine-motor-skills workshop in the gym with Eric—picking up a fork, tying your shoes, catching a ball, etc. These little things are crucial if you want to maintain a perfect disguise once we've escaped this place! Speaking of which, Harold needs your help."

She nodded toward Mr. Derleth (whose first name wasn't Harold). He put down the scissors he had been using to prune a potted gardenia and rose slowly to his feet, shedding a pair of gardening gloves.

"I know who that is!" Cordelia whispered. "The gardener! I followed him in the halls once and thought he disappeared, only maybe he didn't. Maybe he hid inside Mr. Derleth." Cordelia hissed through her teeth, feeling stupid. "How didn't I know?"

"It's not your fault," Benji said. "They fooled me too. It's not exactly something you think of. 'Hey, my teacher's being weird! Maybe there's a ghost inside them.'"

"Not in a normal school. But here? I should have thought of it. But it never occurred to me that the ghosts would do anything so awful. I thought they were good. I thought—"

"Shh," Benji said, squeezing her hand. "Let's see

what your gardener has to say."

Harold stepped to the front of the room and cleared his throat. He clearly wasn't as comfortable with public speaking as Ms. Dunsworth.

"Afternoon," he said with Mr. Derleth's voice. "I'm looking to round up a group to test the doors and windows of the . . ."

This set off a collective groan from the teachers.

"I know we've done it before!" Harold exclaimed, with a very un-Mr. Derleth like sneer. "But it's like checking for holes in a fence. Maybe there's a break we missed."

"Come on, Harold," Mr. Terpin said, slouching in his seat like a bored teenager (which he might very well have been). "You know that ain't true. Ghosts can't leave this place. Makes no matter if we're in a body or out of a body. This is a prison either way."

"For now," Ms. Dunsworth said, squeezing Harold's shoulder as she took charge again. "But it doesn't hurt to be diligent while we wait for our real escape route. I'll be very disappointed if no one participates."

The teachers nodded like scolded children. Cordelia had a feeling that Harold would have quite a few volunteers to help him after all. She remembered her father telling her once how there were two types of leaders: those who ruled through respect, and those who ruled through fear.

She could tell what type of leader Ms. Dunsworth was.

"A number of new spirits have arrived in the school since our last meeting," Ms. Dunsworth said, consulting her Post-it note again. "I'll need five or six volunteers to greet them. They're bound to be confused at this point, so I would just keep it simple: 'You have two choices. You can stay dead forever, or you can live again in a brand-new body.' Let that sink in for a day or two before you offer them a Brightkey. The smart ones will join us. And the ones who choose their Brights instead?" She scoffed. "Weaklings! We don't want them anyway."

"I'm more than happy to help," Ms. Meeker said. She was a pretty fifth-grade teacher who, when not possessed, sang the national anthem at school assemblies. "But some of those Brightkeys are a pain to figure out. Why'd those kids stop all their rescue attempts? That made everything so much easier!"

"Cordelia Liu and the Núñez boy served a valuable purpose while our numbers were still low," Ms. Dunsworth admitted. "But we can handle recruitment on our own at this point. Right now, I want to keep them as far from us as possible. Otherwise they might get suspicious."

"Too late, loser," Benji said.

Ms. Meeker raised her hand again. "But they can

see us," she said. "Wouldn't it be easier to just . . . get rid of them?"

Cordelia was glad to see that this suggestion made some of the ghosts uncomfortable. "They're just children!" she heard someone say.

"I appreciate your enthusiasm," Ms. Dunsworth said. "But the Matheson girl refused to design our new dehaunter unless I swore that her friends would remain safe. If she fails—or tells her friends the truth—that's a completely different story. But until then, leave those children alone."

Benji gasped. "That's why Agnes is helping them!" he exclaimed. "They threatened to hurt us! She had no choice!"

"Poor Agnes," Cordelia said.

"And poor us if she doesn't come through," Benji added.

"You really think this new dehaunter will work?" Mr. Langan asked. "Because last time—"

"Was a test, nothing more," Mr. Derleth said. "We weren't sure exactly what it was going to do. But this time around, Matheson is building exactly what we want. A dehaunter that will take us straight to freedom in our brand-new bodies."

There was a long round of applause. When it finally died down, Mr. Bruce raised a hand. "This might be nothing, but I saw Benji and Cordelia talking to each other," he said. "They looked thick as thieves, like they were planning something."

Ms. Schwerin chortled. "I know they can see us, but they're still just kids. What can they really do?"

Ms. Dunsworth tapped Dr. Roqueni's temple.

"I've seen what they can do," she said. "They defeated a powerful enemy last year who made the mistake of underestimating them. Let's not fall into the same trap. I'll assign a few guards to keep an eye on them at all times. And if we find that they're poking their noses where they don't belong"—her lips curled into a sinister grin—"Shadow School can always use another ghost or two."

"Yay!" exclaimed Ms. Meeker, clapping her hands.

Ms. Dunsworth gave her a smile of approval before returning her gaze to the teachers at large. "That's all I have for you today," she said, "so I think it's time to split into groups and get to—"

"Excuse me," said Ms. Jackson, raising her hand. "I have a question."

Ms. Dunsworth's shoulders slumped. "Of course you do," she said. "What is it this time?"

"Does anyone else feel kind of bad about this? I mean, these bodies aren't ours. We're stealing them. And, sometimes, if I listen really carefully, I swear I can hear the woman inside me *screaming. . . .*"

Cordelia saw a few teachers roll their eyes, like kids tired of hearing the same boring speech from their parents. But there were a good number who looked guilty as well.

"I know it isn't fair, what happened to us," Ms. Jackson said. "No one wants to die. But that doesn't make this right. These bodies belong to good people. They don't deserve this."

The teachers waited for Ms. Dunsworth to reply. She smiled patiently and stuck her hand beneath the spout of a stone fountain. "You're right," Ms. Dunsworth said, watching in fascination as water flowed over her fingers. "They don't deserve this. *We* do. The only way to truly appreciate sensation is to be deprived of it. These 'good people,' as you call them, take it all for granted, staring down at their phones when they should be treasuring every minute of their precious, fragile existence. Living is wasted on them. But not on us, my friends. We understand. We value."

The ghosts nodded their teacher masks in agreement.

Ms. Jackson looked around at them, shaking her head. "But this is wrong," she said. "Why don't you understand?"

"Enough," Dr. Roqueni said. She nodded toward

Mr. Bruce, who pushed the A/V cart toward the front of the conservatory. Cordelia could see the unbridled fear on the teachers' faces as the cart went by. Several of the ghosts slipped out of their hosts for a moment, perhaps resisting the urge to flee, before regaining their composure.

"I should have gone into my Bright when I had the chance," Ms. Jackson said.

"Too late now," Ms. Dunsworth replied.

She removed the black sheet from the cart, revealing the architectural model that Cordelia had knocked from its pedestal. There was an audible gasp of horror from the audience. The ghost inside Ms. Jackson leaped out of her body: a young woman with pigtails and hiking boots. Before she could float away, a few ghosts from the window floated over and grabbed her.

Meanwhile, Ms. Jackson's body slouched over, unoccupied, and an ambitious ghost seized the opportunity and possessed her. Obviously the ghost didn't have much experience, because she could barely manage to maneuver Ms. Jackson to an empty seat. It was enough for now.

"Put her hand on the roof," Dr. Roqueni said, backing away in order to keep her distance from the house. "And make sure none of you are touching the trap yourself when it goes off."

The ghosts pinned the hiker's hand to the roof while Mr. Derleth knelt next to the house and pressed the tiny doorbell. A bell tolled, its low knell reverberating throughout the conservatory, and a layer of the ghost transformed into dust and swept down the chimney. Faded now, mouth wide in a soundless scream, the hiker tried to jerk her hand away. Her captors held her fast. The bell tolled for a second time, and another layer vanished down the chimney, leaving a ghost that was barely visible at all.

After the third toll, there was nothing left.

Mr. Derleth replaced the black sheet, and Mr. Bruce pushed the cart out of the conservatory. Only then did Dr. Roqueni speak again.

"I hope this serves as a reminder to all of you. I've given you a second chance at life. But I can take it away just as easily." She offered them a frosty smile. "Now go out into this prison of ours and do your jobs. Learn. Practice. Recruit. We only have a few weeks before the new dehaunter is complete—the *right* dehaunter, this time. We must be ready. The world awaits."

17

Reunion

After they snuck out of the school, Benji's dad drove them to Cordelia's house. They would have gone to Benji's house, but they needed to talk in private, and his sisters never left them alone.

Cordelia's mom was standing at the sink, rinsing off vegetables. "Benji," she said. "It's been a while."

Mrs. Liu liked Benji and usually took great pleasure in teasing Cordelia about him. But this time, there was something strained about her smile.

"Hi, Mrs. Liu," Benji said. "It's nice to see you."

"You too. Actually, I was running some errands last week and I saw you through the window of the ice cream shop. You were with someone. I thought it might

178

have been Cordelia at first, but it was actually some other girl. Long hair? Very pretty."

Benji swallowed nervously. "That was my friend Vivi."

Mrs. Liu wiped her hands on a dishtowel. "Vivi. What a lovely name."

"We have homework," Cordelia said, dragging Benji away. They went down to the basement, where they usually hung out. It was little more than a couple of cheap sofas, an old TV, and a pile of board games—but it had played host to a lot of fun afternoons.

"Why does your mom hate me now?" Benji asked, taking his usual seat.

"Sorry," Cordelia replied, pacing. "I've been bummed lately with everything that's going on. And she has this stupid idea that me and you are like, a thing. So when she saw you with another girl . . . forget it. She's just being a mom."

"She thinks I dumped you for Vivi?" Benji asked.

Cordelia shook her head. "She knows we're not dating. I wouldn't hide that from her. She probably just thinks—I don't know. You like Vivi better than me?"

Cordelia hadn't intended to phrase it in the form of a question, but there it was, lingering in the air like an unpopped bubble. She bit her lower lip, waiting for Benji's response. He opened his mouth, as though he were about to say something, then closed it and shoved his hands into his pockets. "So this is crazy," he said, plunking his feet on the coffee table. "With the ghosts."

Cordelia took a seat on the sofa across from him. "Where do we even start?" she asked.

"Ms. Dunsworth. If we can figure out who she is, maybe we can figure out her Brightkey. I know she won't take it. Not voluntarily. But maybe we can make her."

Cordelia nodded. "I thought of that too. So I tried googling her in the car. Dead end. We don't know her first name, for one thing. And just because she's a ghost doesn't mean she was anyone special when she was alive—which was a really long time ago, by the way."

"Yeah, she said she was what? A hundred and fifty years old? Something's off about that. If she's been hanging around Shadow School this entire time, why haven't we seen her?"

"I don't know," Cordelia said. The ghosts they rescued all wore relatively modern clothing from the time when they were alive. Someone wearing clothes from the nineteenth century would have stuck out like a sore thumb.

But what if Ms. Dunsworth isn't a normal ghost from Shadow School, Cordelia thought, retuning to a theory that had been bouncing around her head since they'd left the school. *What if she's a ghost from somewhere else?*

"The house I broke," Cordelia said. "You saw what it did to the ghost possessing Ms. Jackson."

"Sucked her inside," Benji said. "Which is a new level of crazy, by the way."

"It *trapped* her inside," Cordelia said. "The house is like a mini Shadow School. A prison for ghosts. Which means it was like that before I broke it, too."

Benji sat forward, mouth agape. "You set Dunsworth free. Like a genie in a bottle. Except with possession instead of wishes."

"It fits," Cordelia said. "Remember that journal Agnes showed us? Elijah got paid to get rid of the ghosts in those old houses. What if he didn't use Brightkeys like we do? What if he trapped them instead, by sucking them into his little houses?"

"That's why we haven't seen Dunsworth before this," Benji said. "And why she's so old."

Cordelia sank into the sofa and covered her face.

"She would have stayed there forever if I hadn't knocked the house over and set her free. Ugh! This is all my fault!"

"Because you're a klutz?"

"Because I was *mean*," Cordelia said. "If we had given that trick-or-treater her Brightkey from the start, I never would have backed into the house to begin with."

"Fine. It's *our* fault. Stop being a blame hog. We got into this together. And we're going to get out of it together."

Benji came over and sat next to her on the couch. For a moment, Cordelia thought he was going to put his arm around her. But instead he just sat there. That was nice too.

"Thank you for being so sweet," Cordelia said. "But this is different than anything we've ever faced before. This isn't just saving ghosts. This is saving real live people." She ran her hands through her hair. "I wish Agnes was here."

The basement door opened. Agnes appeared at the top of the stairs.

"Wish for a million dollars!" Benji exclaimed, jumping from his seat. "Or pizza. Quick!"

"Hey guys," Agnes said. "Mind if I come down?"

Cordelia blinked, wondering if she was imagining things.

"Benji texted me," Agnes continued as she took the first few steps. "He told me that you snuck into a faculty meeting. You saw the ghosts."

"That's who you were texting in the car?" Cordelia asked Benji. "I thought it was Vivi!"

"Actually, it was both of them," Benji said. "Lightning thumbs!"

"That was super dangerous," Agnes said, nearing the bottom of the stairs now. "You could have been caught. But now that you know the truth, there didn't seem much point in staying away anymore. I'm sorry I had to be mean to you. But if I wasn't, they would have—"

Cordelia wrapped her arms around Agnes and hugged her tight.

Agnes giggled. "I should have baked brownies to celebrate," she said.

"We'll make some later," Cordelia said. "Together."

"And I'll eat them," Benji added, looping his long arms around the girls. "Go team."

Agnes and Cordelia spent a few more minutes tearfully apologizing to each other, while Benji found a tennis ball and kicked it around the room. Despite their current predicament, Cordelia couldn't seem to stop smiling.

We're back together again, she thought. *Everything is going to be okay.*

"Tell us your side of it," Cordelia said, flopping her legs across Agnes's lap. "From the beginning."

Agnes leaned over to tie Cordelia's shoelace, which had come undone. After making a meticulous double knot, she began to talk.

"Remember how you said Dr. Roqueni was acting strange after we tested out the dehaunter?" Agnes asked. "You were right. We thought the trial run was a success, because our main goal was getting the ghosts into their Brights. But to Dr. Roqueni—Ms. Dunsworth—it was a complete failure. She has no interest in a peaceful after-life. She wants to leave the school in a fresh new body."

"But she can't just walk out the door," Cordelia said, remembering what she had learned at the meeting. "The rules that keep the ghosts from leaving the school still apply, even if they're hiding in someone's body."

"Exactly," Agnes said. "Ms. Dunsworth was hoping that Elijah's dehaunter would create a portal that allowed ghosts to escape Shadow School and enter the outside world. When she discovered that it took ghosts to their Brights instead, she changed to plan B. For that she needed me. Since I was able to finish the first dehaunter, she figured I'd be able to design a new one that did exactly what she wanted. But she knew she couldn't just pretend to be Dr. Roqueni and ask me, 'Hey—can you build a dehaunter that lets all the ghosts escape?' I would definitely get suspicious. So instead she destroyed the old dehaunter and said that if I didn't build them a new one"—Agnes's eyes found Cordelia and Benji—"'something bad' would happen to you two. I didn't have any choice. I *had* to help her."

"You definitely made the right choice," Benji said. "I'm a big fan of bad things not happening to me."

"So it was Ms. Dunsworth who destroyed the dehaunter," Cordelia said, stroking her chin. "Interesting. And not, you know, a particular person who might have been blamed for destroying the dehaunter. Not thinking of anyone in particular."

"Sorry," Benji said.

"Sorry," Agnes said. "Ms. Dunsworth made me say you were the one who did it. She knows about us stopping the ghost snatchers last year and wanted to make sure we stayed out of the picture. She already had me under her control, and she figured if you and Benji stopped talking to each other our entire group would fall apart." Agnes turned to Cordelia, blushing furiously. "That's why I had to say all those mean things to you that morning. Ms. Dunsworth was in Dr. Roqueni's body, watching. If I didn't sell it . . ."

"You were trying to protect us," Cordelia said, giving her a hug. "I forgive you. But if the whole super genius thing doesn't work out, I think Hollywood is calling your name."

"I was a pretty amazing pumpkin number two in my second-grade play," Agnes said. "My mom still talks about it."

"Let's get back to this new and unimproved

dehaunter," Benji said. "If this thing works, and the ghosts escape the school in our teachers' bodies, what happens to our real teachers? Will the ghosts ever let them be . . . them again? Or is that it? Dr. Roqueni is Dunsworth forever?"

"I don't know," Agnes said. "And even if the ghosts do leave the teachers—what's to stop them from hopping into someone else's body instead? Now that they know how to possess people, they're way too dangerous."

"We can't let them leave the school," Cordelia said. "Period."

"No worries," Benji said, leaning forward with his hands clasped together. "Knowing Agnes, she has some sort of brilliant plan up her sleeve. What is it? Have you been designing a fake dehaunter?"

"Not exactly."

"I know!" Benji exclaimed, raising a finger in the air. "It's a dehaunter that's actually a ghost bomb that will blow them all up the moment you activate it!"

"That's not a thing."

"So what's the plan?" Benji asked.

Agnes looked nervously from Benji to Cordelia.

"So what I've been doing," she said, "is sort of, you know, designing exactly what Ms. Dunsworth wants. That's the first part."

Cordelia and Benji waited.

"I haven't actually figured out the second part yet," Agnes said quietly.

"That's okay," Cordelia said. "We'll work it out."

"You know what the worst part is?" Agnes asked. "I keep expecting Dr. Roqueni to help us. Every time I see her, my first inclination is, *She'll get us out of this!* Then I remember that it isn't Dr. Roqueni anymore. We're on our own."

Cordelia planted a palm in her forehead, wondering why she hadn't thought of it earlier.

"What?" Benji asked.

"I know someone who can help us," she said. "But you're not going to like it."

18

Ms. Dunsworth's Story

That Saturday, Cordelia, Benji, and Agnes walked into Moose Scoops, Ludlow's ice cream shop. It was about as empty as you would expect an ice cream shop to be during a December afternoon in New Hampshire. The teenager sitting behind the counter looked annoyed that his quality phone time was being interrupted by actual customers. His tag read: *SAWYER. MY FAVORITE FLAVOR IS RUM RAISIN.*

"You picking up the birthday cake?" he asked.

Cordelia shook her head.

"You sure?" Sawyer asked. "Someone ordered a birthday cake. It says 'Happy Birthday, Lisa.' I wrote it myself."

"It's not us," Benji said. "We don't even know any Lisas."

"Speak for yourself," Agnes said. "I met a Lisa at science camp two years ago. Really nice girl. I thought we might become friends, but all she wanted to do was talk about butterflies. There's only so much you can say about larvae and proboscises." Agnes saw the eager look in Sawyer's eyes and added, "It's not my cake, though. I don't even know when Butterfly Lisa's birthday is."

Sawyer sighed dramatically. "Then why are you here?"

"We're meeting someone," Cordelia said.

It seemed rude not to order anything, so they each got a scoop of ice cream (cookies and cream for Benji, chocolate brownie with walnuts for Agnes, strawberry for Cordelia) and took a seat at the back table. Darius Shadow showed up a few minutes later. After a brief exchange in which he assured Sawyer that he was not there for a birthday cake, he made his way to their table, blowing into his hands for warmth.

"I find it hard to believe that people would voluntarily choose to live here," he said, removing his overcoat and laying it carefully over his chair. "Penguins, maybe. But not people."

"Not all penguins live in cold climates," Agnes said.

189

"There's actually one species that lives on the Galápagos Islands."

Darius sat down and gave Agnes an amused look. "And who are you, exactly?"

"My name is Agnes Matheson, Mr. Shadow. It's a pleasure to meet you." She reached out and shook his hand.

"Polite," Darius said. "That's refreshing in your generation." He nodded toward Benji. "The boy from the attic, correct?"

"Benji."

"All right, then," Darius said, rubbing his hands together. "You were very convincing on the phone, Cordelia. 'We need to talk to you. It's a matter of life and death!' Now what's this all about?"

Cordelia took a deep breath. Dr. Roqueni had warned her not to trust her uncle. But Dr. Roqueni wasn't here. And they needed all the help they could get. "I can see ghosts," she said.

"Me too," added Benji.

"Not me," Agnes said. "But I do have these special—"

Cordelia nudged her leg beneath the table. They needed Darius's help, but that didn't mean they had to tell him *everything*.

"I see," Darius said, folding his arms across his

chest. If he was surprised by their revelation, he was doing a good job hiding it. "Let's assume I believe you. Why are you telling me this?"

"Because Dr. Roqueni needs your help, and we don't know anyone else who knows about the ghosts except you," Cordelia said. "Remember how you said she wasn't acting like herself last summer? You were right. She's possessed. Most of our teachers are."

"And we were thinking, since you're, like, a ghost expert," Benji said, "you've probably seen this sort of thing before. So maybe you know a special way to stop them. Is there something that will keep ghosts from jumping into a person's body? What about garlic?"

"That's vampires," Agnes whispered.

"Or holy water?"

"Still vampires."

"Or silver?"

"Werewolves," Agnes said. "And sometimes vampires."

"Exactly," Benji said, snapping his fingers. "Like those things, but to stop ghosts from possessing people."

Darius stared at them, dumbfounded. "Ghosts can possess people?"

"His answer doesn't fill me with confidence," Agnes said.

"Is Aria in some kind of danger?" Darius asked.

"Big-time," Cordelia said. "We were hoping you could help."

Darius pulled his chair closer to the table. Its feet scraped against the floor. "Tell me more," he said.

"Give us a second," Cordelia said.

She pulled her friends to the other side of the store for a whisper-filled huddle. They had initially planned to tell Darius as little as possible, but now she wondered if they should reconsider that plan. Even though Dr. Roqueni didn't trust him, he seemed willing to help— and time was running out. They needed to take some chances if they were going to stop Ms. Dunsworth.

In the end, they decided to keep Elijah's office and the spectercles a secret for now, but told Darius about everything else, including the two dehaunters and Ms. Dunsworth's plan to escape with the teachers' bodies.

Darius listened with growing horror. "We have to get Aria out of there," he said, reaching for his coat. "Now. The ghosts can't cross the threshold. So if I can manage to drag her out the front door, this Ms. Dunsworth will be forced to leave her body."

"That doesn't help any of the other teachers," Cordelia said.

Darius shrugged. "Aria comes first. Once she's safe, we'll worry about everyone else."

"There're too many of them," Agnes said. "They'll stop you. Or worse. They'll make you one of them."

"You three seem fine," Darius pointed out.

"The ghosts don't possess kids," Benji said.

"Why not?" Darius asked with genuine curiosity. "If I was a ghost, I'd want the youngest body possible. You'd live longer that way."

"That's a good point," Agnes said.

"It doesn't matter," Benji said. "Just stay away from the school. If you get caught, the game's up. Dunsworth will know we're onto her. And right now, the only advantage we have is surprise."

"Well, there must be *something* I can do!" Darius exclaimed. A pleading look came into his eyes. "Please. Let me help her."

Cordelia couldn't help feeling bad for the old man. Maybe Dr. Roqueni was wrong about him. As far as she could tell, all he wanted to do was save her.

"What about the house in the attic?" Darius asked. "If what you say is true, and Ms. Dunsworth once lived there—I know its story. Grandma Wilma told it to me when I was a little boy."

The three kids exchanged excited glances.

"That could definitely be helpful," Agnes said.

"Your grandma told you about Dunsworth?" Benji asked.

"Grandma Wilma told me about the ghost that haunted that house," Darius said. "I don't recollect if she ever told me the name, but if you say it was this Ms. Dunsworth, that works for me. In my defense, it wasn't a very memorable ghost. Just another vengeful spirit, like all those old ones."

"Actually," Cordelia said, "most of the ghosts I've met are very nice."

"How can you still think that?" Benji asked. "They want to steal our teachers' bodies!"

"It's not them. It's this Ms. Dunsworth. She has them brainwashed or something."

"Seriously, Cordelia? You honestly think–"

"Shh," Agnes said, reaching out and squeezing their arms. "Let the nice man talk."

Darius looked from Benji to Cordelia and gave them that knowing grin that grown-ups sometimes did, like they clearly liked each other but hadn't figured it out yet.

"The ghosts in Shadow School are harmless," Darius said. "For the most part. But that's only because they haven't been dead very long. Leave them there long enough, and they'll start to go bad. It's inevitable."

"Why?" Agnes asked.

Darius held up a finger, then quickly snatched a napkin from the dispenser on the table and sneezed. "Let me ask you a question," he said, wiping his nose. "Have you ever been so jealous of someone else it makes your blood boil?"

Cordelia pictured Vivi playfully messing up Benji's hair as they stood by his locker.

"I think I can imagine that," she said.

"Well, multiply that feeling by a million, and now you know what a ghost feels like," Darius said. "Imagine being trapped in a world where you're cold all the time and can't touch anything or talk to anyone. Pretty awful. But what if you were also surrounded by people who can do all the things you miss the most—laughing, talking, eating—and all you can do is watch them? It might take a decade or two, but even if you were the kindest person on earth when you were alive, you'd start to wonder how come they get to live and you don't. How is that fair?" He tapped the table with a single finger. "No good can come from jealousy. For the living or the dead. Marinate in those dark feelings long enough, and jealousy becomes hatred; hatred becomes evil. Every good ghost is a bad ghost waiting to happen. It's just a matter of time."

Cordelia was reminded of something they had learned months ago: when ghosts got older, they transformed into "phantoms," developing special abilities or turning monstrous in appearance. *Maybe it's jealousy of the living that causes them to change,* Cordelia thought. She wondered if any of the other architectural models in the attic contained phantoms, and what they might be like. A cold sweat broke out across the back of her neck.

"How did Ms. Dunsworth die?" Agnes asked, bringing Cordelia back to the conversation at hand.

"I don't recall," Darius said. "It wasn't anything special, like she was murdered and refused to rest until she took her revenge. That kind of stuff only happens in the movies. She just died. A new family moved into the house. At first, everything was okay. Nice, even. Ms. Dunsworth banged some pots or slammed a door now and then, but for the most part she was a good ghost. Helpful. Lost objects would suddenly reappear on the kitchen table. And there was a baby girl who always kicked off her blankets in the middle of the night. Yet every morning her blanket would be back in place."

Cordelia imagined a woman in an old-fashioned gown standing over a crib, watching a baby sleep. Perhaps Ms. Dunsworth's intentions had been good at this point, but the image still sent a chill down her spine.

"The real problems started with the second family that moved into the house," Darius said. "By this point, jealousy of the living had blackened Ms. Dunsworth's heart. She didn't help this family. She terrorized them. Her biggest trick was appearing in the mirror when they were checking their reflection and miming their movements."

"She wanted to be them," Cordelia said, remembering the way Martha, the old woman who walked into their science class, had imitated Vivi before trying to possess her.

Darius nodded. "That family moved out quick," he said. "They were smart. But the next group was determined to stick it out no matter what." He shook his head. "There was a series of 'accidents,' one after another. I'll spare you the details. Eventually, only the mother remained. She's the one who called Elijah, who finally drove Ms. Dunsworth from the house."

A somber silence fell over the table. Cordelia poked at her ice cream with her spoon. It had melted into a sweet soup.

"Do you remember any other details about Ms. Dunsworth?" Agnes asked. "What she wore? How she looked? Anything that might have seemed important to her when she was alive?"

"Sorry, kids," Darius said, leaning back in his seat. "That's all I've got."

Benji got to his feet and started putting his coat on. "We better head home," he said, nodding toward the window. The sky had gotten appreciably darker since their arrival. "It's going to snow soon."

"What are you going to do?" Darius asked.

"We'll think of something," Agnes said.

"I want to help."

Cordelia shook her head. "We appreciate it. But there's nothing you can do."

"Because I can't see the ghosts," Darius said through gritted teeth. "Useless as always. Story of my life." He took a breath, steadying himself. "Well, there's a dinky little motel just down the road. I'll be there until Aria is safe and sound. You know my number. You figure out a way I can help—any way at all—you give me a call."

"Thanks," Cordelia said. She doubted they'd be able to use his help, but she still appreciated the offer. And after everything was done, she made a promise to herself that she would convince Dr. Roqueni to give him another chance. Maybe he hadn't been the best uncle when she was a kid, but it seemed like he had changed since then.

"You're okay, Mr. Shadow," Benji said.

"You too," he replied with a smile. "Be careful. All of you."

They each shook his hand and started to bundle up. By the time they were done, the snow had begun to fall. Cordelia tucked her hair beneath her hood, ready to brave the storm.

The Two Passageways

At school, Cordelia tried to become invisible. She didn't raise her hand in class, sat by herself at lunch, and completely ignored Benji and Agnes. The ghost in the blue prom dress had been assigned to guard her, and Cordelia wanted to put on a good show. Things would be easier if Ms. Dunsworth believed that she had completely given up.

When Cordelia wasn't in school, it was a different story.

She stayed up late every night, texting her friends. If they put their minds together, she knew they'd find a way to stop the ghosts. Their initial idea was to catch Dr. Roqueni or Mr. Derleth outside the walls of Shadow

School, when they weren't possessed, and explain what was going on. Unfortunately, Dr. Roqueni slept in her apartment every night and ordered groceries delivered to the school, and as far as they could tell, Mr. Derleth was staying there as well. Darius Shadow even tried calling his niece to convince her to go out to dinner, but she wouldn't go for it.

At the end of January, the flu danced through the halls, dragging partners away at random. Empty chairs outnumbered occupied ones. Benji got sick, then Cordelia, then Agnes. By the time they were well again, the school had been invaded by paper hearts stapled to bulletin boards and dangling from red yarn hung across classroom ceilings. Cordelia thought she saw Benji and Vivi holding hands as they walked down the hall. She decided not to ask him about it.

Then Ludlow was hit hard by the worst nor'easter in a decade, and they had three glorious snow days in a row.

The storm stalled progress on the dehaunter, but unfortunately this only made Ms. Dunsworth more impatient to complete it. She warned Agnes that if the plans weren't done by the end of the month, it would be her friends who paid the price.

Knowing that they had to figure out an answer fast, they started to consider ideas that might have previously seemed outlandish. The cart that the ghost snatchers had used to dispose of their quarry lay beneath a tarp in Elijah's office. Could they possibly make use of it? And then there was the horseshoe house. If they could somehow pin Dr. Roqueni's hand to the roof and press the doorbell, would it imprison Ms. Dunsworth just as it had the ghost in the faculty meeting?

They balanced the ifs and coulds against the possible consequences if they failed and decided that they hadn't yet come upon a solution likely enough to succeed. When the end of February arrived, Agnes had no choice but to give Ms. Dunsworth her completed plans for the dehaunter. The ghosts had a carpenter among their ranks, but the plans were complex. It would be at least six weeks before the dehaunter was finished.

If they didn't think of a solution before then, all was lost.

By this point, Cordelia suspected that the ghosts were no longer lingering in the background and had taken full control of all their teachers. It was a horrible thought. On the other hand, it meant that her "teachers" had stopped assigning homework, so it wasn't all bad. Cordelia was making good use of this free time by watching random YouTube videos on her Chromebook when her cell phone started to buzz.

Agnes wanted to FaceTime her.

"Hey," Cordelia said, answering the call. Agnes's face appeared, looking scrunched in the tiny screen.

"What are you doing right now?" Agnes asked.

Cordelia glanced over the phone at the video currently streaming on her Chromebook. A kitten was attempting to knock down a Christmas ornament from the lower branches of a tree.

"Research," she said.

"You're watching cat videos again, aren't you?"

"Maybe."

"That's cool. I think I've figured out a way to stop the ghosts. But if you're too busy right now . . ."

Cordelia sat up and slammed her Chromebook shut.

"I'm all ears," she said. "You want me to call Benji?"

"I texted him. He can't talk right now. He's with Vivi."

"Of course he is."

"They're bowling."

"I don't need to know," Cordelia said. "Tell me your plan."

Even in the tiny screen, Cordelia could see the excitement in Agnes's eyes.

"Remember the day we were checking those wires? I turned the triangle and made the purple light, and mentioned it was a different color in the other passageway?"

"Green, right?"

"Correct," Agnes said. "Well, I didn't know it at the time, but it turns out the colors are different because the pyramids in one passageway are producing a completely different type of energy than the other pyramids. The purple energy sends ghosts into their Brights. The green energy, on the other hand, opens up portals that will let the ghosts leave the school. I don't think Elijah was sure which set of pyramids was going to work. So he built both of them."

There was a knock at Cordelia's door.

"Your mom and I are playing Yahtzee," said Mr. Liu, inching the door open a respectful few inches. "You want to play?"

"Not tonight. Thanks."

"We made popcorn."

"Test tomorrow! Gotta study."

Cordelia made sure her father's footsteps had retreated down the stairs before continuing her conversation.

"I'm confused," she said. "If the pyramids are supplying all the energy, then what does the dehaunter do?"

"It changes the raw energy into a form the mirrors can actually use," Agnes said. "The original dehaunter absorbed the purple energy, transferred it into what

203

Elijah called 'activation mist,' and sent it up to the mirrors. That's why the Brights appeared when we tested it out. The one I designed for Ms. Dunsworth does the same thing but pulls from the green energy pyramids instead."

"Just like she wants," Cordelia said. "I don't understand how this helps us."

"Because the dehaunter I built is different from the first one," Agnes said. "It's compatible with both types of energy. It uses the portal pyramids by default. But let's say that green energy isn't available. I designed the dehaunter so that instead of turning off, it just switches to the nearest available energy source. In other words, if we can somehow manage to turn off the portal pyramids—"

"The dehaunter will use the purple energy instead and send the ghosts into their Brights!" Cordelia exclaimed. "This is brilliant! Why did you wait so long to tell us?"

"Because I just figured out the last part tonight. It's not as easy as it sounds, Cord. Ms. Dunsworth is definitely going to test the dehaunter before she turns it on full blast. So it has to work the way she wants, at least the first time."

"No problem," Cordelia said. "We let her test it so she believes you did what she wants. Then we turn off the portal pyramids. When she powers up the dehaunter to use it for real, it'll send all the ghosts to their Brights before she realizes anything's wrong."

"I was thinking the same thing," Agnes said. "But there's one huge problem—"

Someone knocked on Cordelia's door.

"What?" Cordelia asked.

"Did your dad tell you we're playing Yahtzee?" Mrs. Liu asked.

"I'm busy!"

"There's popcorn."

"I can't! This is the biggest test of my life! I have to study!"

"There's no need to be dramatic," Mrs. Liu said. "I'll leave you a bowl of popcorn on the kitchen table."

She left.

"Your parents are so cute," Agnes said. "If they were our age, I'd want to be friends with them."

"So what's the problem?" Cordelia asked.

"Turning off the portal pyramids isn't as easy as flipping an on/off switch," Agnes said. "It's more like . . . disarming a bomb. There are a dozen steps that have to be done in a specific order, or the energy might escape. That would be bad."

"How bad?"

"Big-boom bad," Agnes said.

Cordelia shook her head. It was always something. "Can't you just figure it out?" she asked. "You're Agnes!"

"Not this time," Agnes said. "I need Elijah's original directions. There's no other way. And guess where those are?"

"His office," Cordelia said. She rubbed a hand over her face. "How do you expect us to sneak down there? You know how cautious Dunsworth is being. The ghosts are watching every move we make."

Agnes grinned. "You're right," she said. "That's why we're going to need some help."

20

Trust

Cordelia sat in her basement, unhappily eating a corn chip. In the last fifteen minutes, she had gone through an entire bowl of them. She didn't even like corn chips.

"I have concerns," she said, checking the basement door. Their visitors would be there any minute.

"Yeah," Benji replied. "I think you were pretty clear about that the first ten thousand times. But I'm telling you, this is the best plan. Agnes? Isn't this the best plan?"

"If by 'best' you mean 'only,' then I totally agree," Agnes said.

"We all know why Benji likes it," Cordelia muttered.

"Seriously?" Benji asked.

The doorbell rang. Cordelia heard her mother answer the door and an exchange of pleasantries. A few moments later, Ezra came down the stairs, wearing his backpack as though this was just another day of school.

"Hey, dude," Benji said, offering him a fist bump. Ezra awkwardly took Benji's entire hand in his own and attempted to shake it.

"Thank you for inviting me," Ezra said to Cordelia. "My mom wasn't going to let me go at first, because you're a seventh grader and she doesn't know anything about you, but then she googled your parents and didn't find anything too objectionable, so she finally changed her mind." He gave an apologetic shrug. "I'm sorry about the questionnaire. Mom makes all my friends' parents fill that out."

"It's okay," Cordelia said. "I'm glad you could make it."

Ezra took off his backpack. "I brought seaweed crackers. And Jenga!"

The doorbell rang. Cordelia heard footsteps as someone went to answer the door—her father this time. Judging from the muffled voices coming from the kitchen, Mrs. Liu was still trapped in a conversation with Ezra's mom.

A few moments later, Vivi came down the stairs

with a befuddled expression on her face, as though she wasn't sure exactly what she was doing there. She burst into a smile the moment she saw Benji, however. He shifted over on the couch, making room for her.

Ignoring the sudden ache in her stomach—*too many corn chips*—Cordelia focused on the reason she had brought them all together.

"Okay," she said, pacing back and forth. "I'm sure you've both noticed that Shadow School is not exactly a normal public school, but it's even stranger than you think. I'm going to tell you the truth now. You might be scared. You might think we're crazy. But all I ask is that you hear me out. We need your help, otherwise I wouldn't be doing—"

"Is this about the ghosts?" Vivi asked.

Cordelia froze. Benji buried his face in his hands.

"How did you know that?" Cordelia managed.

"Benji told me all about them," Vivi said.

Cordelia glared at Benji. "You *told* her?"

"You were supposed to play dumb," Benji muttered to Vivi.

"I don't like lying," said Vivi.

"Did someone say ghosts?" asked Ezra.

"This is unbelievable!" Cordelia said, throwing her hands into the air. "I can't believe you just told her without even asking me first!"

"I didn't realize I had to get permission, Mom," Benji said, growing annoyed. "Vivi is my friend. I didn't plan it. We were just talking, and it came out."

"We're telling her now anyway," Agnes said, trying to defuse the situation. "This just makes it easier."

"Ghosts aren't real," Ezra said, his upper lip quivering.

"Yeah, I didn't believe it at first either," Vivi replied. "Not until Benji let me use the goggles."

Now it was Agnes's turn to look annoyed. "You let her use my spectercles?" she yelled at Benji.

"Spectercles?" Vivi asked.

"Not yours," Benji told Agnes. "One of the extra pairs. I just gave her a little tour, that's all. This was months ago."

Cordelia took a handful of corn chips and shoved them into her mouth. "Is that seriously all the ghosts are to you?" she asked, talking with her mouth full. "A way to impress some girl?"

Vivi got to her feet with a defiant expression.

"I am not 'some girl,'" she said. "And if you really want my help, maybe you should focus on the fact that even after I saw the ghosts, I kept going to school anyway. Lots of other kids would have run screaming and never come back."

"Is that an option?" Ezra asked. At some point he had pulled Drool, the stuffed wolf, out of his backpack and started cradling him in his lap.

"Don't worry," Agnes said, stroking Drool behind the ears. "Most of the ghosts are nice."

"Most?" Ezra asked.

"I'm sorry you don't like me, Cordelia," Vivi said, hands on her hips. "But you said it yourself. You need my help. So what's it going to be? We going to get along or am I going home?"

Cordelia took a steadying breath. "It's not that I don't like *you*, personally," she said.

"I know," Vivi said, her eyes flicking toward Benji. "But do we really want to go there?"

Cordelia felt a bolt of anger. *He was my friend first,* she thought. *Maybe more than friend, if you hadn't gotten in the way!* Before she could say anything that might have sent Vivi—and Benji—storming out of her house, she heard Darius Shadow's voice in her head:

No good can come from jealousy. For the living or the dead.

"I'm glad Benji told you about the ghosts," Cordelia said. "And that you're not scared. This just proves you're the right girl for the job." She smirked at Benji. "Clearly you're a lot braver than this one was when he first started seeing the ghosts."

Vivi grinned. "He told me he was never scared of them! Not even a little bit."

"Ha!" Cordelia exclaimed. "I told you he was trying to impress you."

Both Benji and Vivi blushed. Cordelia felt the same sick feeling in the pit of her stomach, but this time she knew it had nothing to do with corn chips. The worst part was that she was starting to see why Benji liked Vivi so much.

"Is this streaming through the YouTube right now?" Ezra asked. He scanned the basement as though looking for hidden cameras. "Am I being puked?"

"Punked," Benji said. "And no. We're not making anything up."

"Remember the first day of school, how you thought Shadow School was haunted?" Agnes asked. "Yay! You were right!"

Ezra looked like he was ready to cry. "I'm going home," he said, rising from the sofa.

Vivi and Benji pulled him back down.

"Don't worry," Vivi said. "They're not as scary as they sound. They're just people."

"Dead people," Ezra said.

"Well, the good news is that if you help us," Cordelia said, "Shadow School won't be haunted for much longer. I believe in you, Ezra. If you're brave enough to face Mason James, you're brave enough to face a couple of ghosts."

"But I'm *not* brave enough to face Mason James. I run away every time!"

"Perfect!" Cordelia exclaimed. "That's exactly what I want you to do if you see a ghost! Just warn Vivi that they're coming first. She has the dangerous part."

Vivi rubbed her hands together. "Sounds like fun," she said. "What's the plan?"

21

The Plan

As if possessing their social studies teacher wasn't evil enough, the ghost inhabiting Mr. Hearn had decided to give them a pop quiz. Cordelia stared at the screen of her Chromebook, struggling to remember who had been president during the Mexican-American War. Her attention kept wandering to Vivi's empty seat.

She should be back by now, Cordelia thought.

The plan had been for Vivi and Ezra to meet at the basement door at ten a.m. Ezra would use Agnes's spectercles to watch out for ghosts, while Vivi—also wearing spectercles—ran into Elijah's office and snagged the instructions for disabling the pyramids.

The entire trip, start to finish, should have taken ten minutes. Fifteen, tops.

Vivi had been gone for over twenty minutes now.

Something's wrong, Benji wrote on the Google Doc that Cordelia kept open next to her test. **We have to help them.**

We can't, Agnes chimed in. **There are eyes on us, remember?**

Cordelia peeked over the top of the Chromebook. Her own personal guard, the Prom Queen, was leaning against the whiteboard, staring at her nails. Benji's and Agnes's guards were doing a better job of hiding, but Cordelia was certain they were nearby.

Give them a few more minutes, Cordelia wrote.

"Mr. Hearn," Miranda said. "Cordelia's typing messages to someone. I can see it from here."

Mr. Hearn rose from his seat with a dangerous look in his eyes. Cordelia saw the text vanish from her screen as Agnes desperately erased it from her end and began typing something new.

"Keep your hands off that machine," Mr. Hearn ordered Cordelia. He turned his body in order to make his way between the tightly packed desks. "I knew you were up to something! I knew it! Now let's see what kind of secret messages you're writing!"

He spun the Chromebook around triumphantly. The document read:

Hey, Agnes. Can you tell me what manifest destiny is? I know nothing and you're the smartest person in the world.

Go away. I hate you.

"Sorry," Cordelia said, raising her hands into the air. "I was trying to cheat. You got me."

Mr. Hearn slammed the Chromebook shut. As he did, Vivi glided into the room behind him. She gave Benji a quick thumbs-up and took her seat.

She did it! Cordelia thought.

"You look awfully happy for someone who just got a zero on their test," Mr. Hearn said.

"I'm thrilled to have learned the error of my ways," Cordelia said.

Mr. Hearn grunted and returned to his seat.

Cordelia was eager to hear the details of Vivi's and Ezra's adventure, but that would have to wait until they could talk without the risk of being overheard. Their plan had worked. That was the important thing.

It's not over yet, Cordelia thought. *After Ms. Dunsworth tests the dehaunter, we still have to sneak into the pyramid passageway and shut it down.* She smiled to herself. *Of course, that might be a little easier now that our team has two new members.*

In gym, they played Wiffle Ball. In Spanish, they reviewed how to conjugate verbs ending in *-ir.* Dr. Roqueni was waiting for them in science. She stood with her hands clasped behind her back until all the students had taken their seats.

"If it's not too much trouble," she said, giving Ms. Jackson a knowing smile, "could I borrow a few students for a little project I'm doing? Let me see . . ." She took her time looking over the class. "How about Benji Núñez, Agnes Matheson, and Cordelia Liu? Oh–and Viviana Martínez! Don't want to leave her out, do I?"

As Cordelia and her friends rose from their seats, ghosts flooded the room, spreading themselves along the walls like parents visiting the school to observe a lesson. A little boy wearing a backward baseball cap wagged his finger at Cordelia in a *you're-in-trouble-now* gesture.

"Ms. Jackson," Dr. Roqueni continued, her cold eyes never leaving Cordelia's. "In about ten minutes, could you call the office and tell them to make an announcement? All staff should report to the conservatory. We're going to start that evacuation drill a little earlier than expected."

Ms. Jackson gave a squeal of delight. "Oh, how

wonderful!" she exclaimed. "Yes, I'll tell Mrs. Flippin. You can count on me!"

"Come along, children," Dr. Roqueni said.

In the hallway, two lines of ghosts that stretched all the way to the stairwell were pouring into the classrooms. Cordelia shared an uneasy look with Benji and Agnes. There were a lot of things troubling her right now, but first and foremost was the phrase *evacuation drill.*

"Is this about what happened in social studies, Dr. Roqueni?" Cordelia tried. "I shouldn't have cheated, but there's no need to blame–"

"Dr. Roqueni isn't here," she said, her dark eyes boring into Cordelia's. "My name is Adelaide Dunsworth. As you well know."

They marched down to the basement, the four children following the possessed principal in a stunned procession. No one spoke. There didn't seem any point. It was over. The ghosts that had been tasked with spying on them for the past few weeks followed at a respectful distance, just in case one of the kids got any funny ideas about escaping.

When they reached the hallway above Elijah's office, Cordelia noticed a massive armoire leaning against the wall. Strange, but not high on her list of priorities at the given moment. *Why is she bringing us here?* Cordelia wondered. Ms. Dunsworth pressed the hibiscuses, and the floor rose up and split apart. The yawning darkness, which had once held the promise of camaraderie and discovery, terrified Cordelia. She felt like she might never return from it again.

Ms. Dunsworth shoved them down the steps. The moment Cordelia entered the office, Ezra ran into her arms. She held him tight.

"I'm sorry," he said. "I was so stupid. Everything went according to plan. I wore those special glasses and watched out for ghosts, just like you told me to. Only when we were done I forgot to take the glasses off. I guess there's a ghost inside Mrs. King, because she was able to see them." Ezra wiped away a tear with his sleeve. "She snatched the glasses right off my face. Then she called Dr. Roqueni."

"It's my fault," Cordelia said, ruffling Ezra's sweaty hair. "I should have never involved you to begin with."

"You're right," Ms. Dunsworth said with a snide smile. "The sniveling little coward told me your entire plan. I didn't even have to ask very hard. Which reminds me"—she stepped over to Vivi and held out her hand—"I'll take that piece of paper in your pocket."

Vivi shrugged. "I don't know what you're talking about."

Ms. Dunsworth raised her eyebrows. "Oh, you're brave," she said. "How nice. But I hope you're realistic as well. You can either give me what I asked for. Or we can take it."

Harold stepped out from the shadows in the corner of the room. His hair had grown long and shaggy in the past few months. Between that and the wicked gleam in his eyes, the gardener hardly resembled Mr. Derleth at all anymore.

He stood behind Vivi, waiting for orders.

"Vivi," Benji said. "You don't have a choice."

Gritting her teeth, Vivi yanked a yellowed piece of parchment from her pocket and tossed it to Ms. Dunsworth, who unfolded the paper and held it to the light. Cordelia wasn't standing close enough to read the words, but she recognized Elijah's cramped handwriting.

"What is this again?" Ms. Dunsworth asked. "Elijah Shadow's instructions for how to turn off the beautiful machine that will free us?" She turned the paper upside down. "Looks complicated. Certainly nothing you could figure out on your own."

She handed the paper to Harold. "Burn it," she said.

Harold produced a silver lighter and lit a corner of the directions. He let the fire breathe for a few moments, then dropped the paper to the ground and stomped out the flames until nothing but ashes remained.

"Elijah!" Benji screamed, calling out for the ghost. "Where are you, buddy? Some poltergeist superpowers would be really helpful right about now!"

Ms. Dunsworth and Harold exchanged an amused look.

"Elijah can't help you," Ms. Dunsworth said. "He realized what we were planning weeks ago and had the audacity to attack me. Can you imagine that? Traitor to his own kind. We had to make sure it didn't happen again."

"What did you do?" Agnes asked.

A high-pitched screeching noise, like the gears of an ancient clock grinding together after a century of slumber, shook the office. Ezra clapped his hands over his ears. The lights above them flickered and sizzled.

"What was that?" Cordelia asked, looking up.

"Oh no," Agnes said, clasping a hand to her mouth. "I think that was the dehaunter starting to power up. Which means"—the color drained from her cheeks— "they've already finished building it."

Ms. Dunsworth applauded. "It works perfectly, by the way," she said. "I tested it last night. I can't tell you how good it felt to breathe in the cool night air. I was tempted to just leave. But I couldn't abandon my people like that. We have things to do."

"Your *people*?" Benji asked. "You mean ghosts?"

"We're not the ghosts!" Ms. Dunsworth shrieked. "You are! Drifting through your pathetic existence in a mindless haze, barely acknowledging the others around you as you poke your little machines. After you die, you'll understand how precious every single breath is. Then, and only then, will you deserve to live." Ms. Dunsworth nodded as she spoke, as though each word further confirmed the nobility of her cause. "Once we're outside," she continued, "we'll start converting others. It'll be much faster this time. Give my staff a few days, and we can teach any ghost how to possess a human. I've heard that there are quite a few graveyards in the area. That seems like a good place to start."

Cordelia knew she should do something. Run. Hide. Scream. But the chilling implications of Ms. Dunsworth's plan had frozen her in place. *Once the ghosts escape, there'll be no way to stop them. The dead will spread across the world like a virus, possessing the bodies of the living at will.*

A wall speaker hissed to life. "All staff, report to the conservatory," Mrs. Flippin said, her usually warm voice cold and robotic. "I repeat. All staff, report to the conservatory at once. Students, remain in your classrooms and await further instructions."

"The mirrors are on the fourth floor," Benji said. "That's your way out. Why would you send all the teachers down to the conservatory?"

Ms. Dunsworth smiled smugly.

"Have you really not figured it out yet?" she asked. "We're going to the conservatory so we can shed these old husks. That door is reinforced steel. Even after they wake up, your teachers won't be able to get out. Not fast enough, at least. We'll be long gone in our fresh young bodies by then."

As she realized what Ms. Dunsworth intended to do, Cordelia felt not surprise, but a cold acceptance. In the darkest part of her mind, she had always known Ms. Dunsworth's ultimate plan. It had just been too horrible to speak aloud.

"This was never about the teachers," Cordelia said. "They were just practice. It's the students you want."

"Obviously," Ms. Dunsworth said. "Why live in a battered old shack when there're hundreds of brand-new houses available? Speaking of which, I need to go. Faculty meeting." She started toward the stairs, waving Mr. Derleth after her. "Come on, Harold."

Harold refused to move. "I don't want to sound like I'm ungrateful for everything that you've done," he said, bowing his head, "but you promised I could be the first. Remember?"

Ms. Dunsworth patted his arm. "So I did, loyal friend," she said. "And you have more than earned the honor." She waved her hand across the room, taking in Cordelia and her friends. "Which one do you want?"

Harold's eyes passed over the girls and settled on Benji and Ezra. He stroked his chin, considering.

"Stay away from us," Benji said, placing himself in front of Ezra.

The ghost of the old gardener stepped out into the open. As Mr. Derleth's body collapsed to the floor, Harold floated toward Benji and Ezra, arms outstretched. Cordelia could see dirt on the fingers of his gardening gloves.

"Stay away!" Benji repeated.

At the last moment, his instincts overcame his good sense, and Benji tried to push the approaching ghost. His momentum took him straight through the gardener, causing him to stumble and fall.

"Cordelia!" Ezra cried, backing away. "What's happening?"

The boy's voice seemed to wake up something inside Cordelia—some tiny flame that refused to be doused no matter how dire the situation—and she started toward him, determined to do *something*. Before she could get three steps, however, an arm wrapped itself around her chest, keeping her still.

"Watch," Ms. Dunsworth whispered in her ear.

Ezra, his eyes frantically searching the room for a ghost he could not see, began to sniffle. "I don't like this," he said as Harold placed two hands on his shoulders and began to grow dimmer. "I don't like this. I don't like—"

He stopped talking. His eyes went flat as Harold disappeared from behind him.

Ezra blinked. "Tight fit," he said in a more assured voice than the real boy had ever possessed. He circled his arms. "Like a suit of clothes that's a few sizes too small."

"You'll grow into it," Ms. Dunsworth said.

Ezra—now Harold—walked across the office. His shoulders were no longer slouched. He looked up at Ms. Dunsworth.

"You're so tall," he said. "Are you going to possess one of these girls now?"

"Not yet," Ms. Dunsworth said, pinching his cheek. "I need to put a few things in motion first. But don't worry, we'll be back." Her eyes jumped from Cordelia to Vivi to Agnes, lingering on each one in turn. "Decisions, decisions."

Ms. Dunsworth and Harold went up the stairs. As soon as they left, Cordelia heard a huge thump above them. *The armoire,* she thought. *They pushed it over so the floor can't rise and let us out.*

Sure enough, when Benji pulled the lever, there was only a strained grinding. The floor didn't move a single inch.

They were trapped.

22

Trapped!

The first thing they did was check on Mr. Derleth. His breathing was steady, but no matter how hard they tried to wake him up, he refused to stir. Cordelia removed her cardigan and slid it beneath his head.

"That ghost has been inhabiting his body for months now," Agnes said, yanking nervously on her braid. "There's no telling what kind of repercussions there might be, both physically and psychologically. . . ."

"Mr. D will be fine," Benji insisted, with a look that dared Agnes to say otherwise. "He just needs to rest. Right now we have to concentrate on getting out of here before Ms. Dunsworth returns."

"Poor Ezra," Vivi said. "He was so scared."

"We're going to rescue him," Cordelia said. "And everyone else too."

"Mr. Shadow is already on his way," Benji said. "I texted him and told him where the office is."

"How did you manage that?" Agnes asked, impressed.

"Ms. Dunsworth was distracted doing her crazy ghosts-are-going-to-rule-the-world speech. Plus: lightning thumbs!"

"Who's Mr. Shadow?" Vivi asked, a glimmer of hope coming into her eyes.

"He's this old dude that Dr. Roqueni told us not to trust," Benji said. "Honestly, I'm not even sure he'll come."

"Wow," Vivi said. "I feel safer already."

"Well, we can't just stand here waiting around," Agnes said. "I'll see if I can figure out a way to open the door."

"I'll check the Brightkey room," Benji said. "Maybe there's something we can use."

"I'll help," said Vivi. As they went into the other room, Cordelia heard her ask, "What's a Brightkey?"

"That noise we heard," Cordelia said, following Agnes to the steps. "Does that mean they can use the dehaunter?"

"Not yet," Agnes said. "It's still warming up. You know how the dehaunter looks like a house? The energy needs to pass through all three floors, from bottom to top, before it's ready to power the mirrors. On the first floor, the molecules undergo a stabilization process in order to prepare—"

Cordelia squeezed Agnes's arm. "I love you but keep it stupid right now. How much time?"

"Thirty minutes," Agnes said. "That sound the dehaunter makes? When we hear it a second time—bad! When we hear it a third time—worse!"

"Got it," Cordelia said, running up the stairs. Peeking between the gaps of the floorboards, she could make out the chestnut wood of the armoire. She pressed her back against the floor and pushed as hard as she could. It didn't move at all.

"Can we science our way out of this?" Cordelia asked. "Like, use physics to make the armoire move or something?"

"You know science and magic are two different things, right?"

"Now is not the time for Snarky Agnes."

Three pounding noises, like someone slamming their fists against the massive door of a cathedral, echoed through the office.

Vivi screamed.

Cordelia and Agnes ran into the Brightkey room, where Vivi was staring in horror at what looked like a tall wooden closet. A thick-shackled padlock hung from the latch on its side.

"Someone's inside," Vivi whispered, pointing to the box. "They're trying to get out."

The pounding started again, even louder this time. The lock rattled and jumped but maintained its hold.

"This is a ghost box," Agnes told Vivi. "Mr. Ward built it for us before he left, just in case we needed it. It's the only thing that can contain them."

"Mr. Ward?" Vivi asked. "Isn't he the custodian that used to work here?"

"He knew about the ghosts too," Agnes said. "But then he moved to Greece."

"Smart guy," Vivi said.

There was a circular window cut into the door of the ghost box. Standing on his tiptoes, Benji cupped his hands to the glass and looked through it.

"It's so dark," he said. "But there's definitely a ghost in there."

"Vivi," Cordelia whispered. "Remember those special goggles Agnes gave you?"

"Spectercles!" Agnes insisted.

"Put them on," Cordelia said. "Just in case."

Vivi nodded and slipped the spectercles over her eyes. She was breathing heavily, but other than that she seemed to be holding it together well. Cordelia couldn't help being impressed.

"Don't get so close," Vivi whispered to Benji, whose

face was pressed against the window. "Whoever's in there is *not* happy."

The door rattled on its hinges, taking Benji by surprise. He fell backward and would have crashed to the floor if Cordelia and Vivi hadn't righted him.

There was a huge grin on his face. "It's Elijah!" he exclaimed. "Ms. Dunsworth must have trapped him in there. We need to get him out!"

"Why would we want to do that?" Vivi asked. "Isn't he a ghost?"

"The good kind," Cordelia said.

"A poltergeist," Agnes added. "He can move objects with his mind. Which means he can help get us out of here."

"A poltergeist," Vivi said. "Sure. Why not?"

"Check the shelves," Benji said. "There must be something we can use to break this lock."

A few minutes later, Cordelia tracked down a tire iron that she had once offered to a ghost wearing mechanic coveralls. At first she tried breaking the window, but the plate was thick and shatterproof, so instead she dug the flat end of the tire iron between the box and door. Planting her feet, she pushed forward with all her might, trying to pry the door open. When it didn't budge, Agnes squeezed next to her, adding her own strength.

Finally, there was a cracking sound like a branch in

a windstorm, and the door swung open. Elijah stepped out of the box. The architect usually looked calm and composed, but not today. His eyes were rimmed with red and his hair stood on end. Cordelia was glad he was on their side.

"Hey, Mr. Shadow," Cordelia said. "We're in trouble here. There's a ghost inside Dr. Roqueni who's planning to steal all our teachers'—"

Elijah nodded and held a finger over her lips.

"He already knows, remember?" Agnes said. At some point she had slid on her spectercles. "That's why he tried to stop her."

A grinding noise shook the school like the roar of a mechanical dragon. Cordelia grabbed Benji for balance as the office began to shake. Brightkeys rained down from the shelves. Water from a shattered snow globe splattered Cordelia's shoe.

The sound stopped. Cordelia realized how close she was holding Benji and let go of him with an embarrassed smile. She saw Vivi watching them.

"You okay?" Cordelia asked.

"Fine," said Vivi.

"The power's reached the second floor of the dehaunter," Agnes said. "We have to hurry. They'll be able to use it soon."

Cordelia looked up at Elijah. "We need to get out

of here, Mr. Shadow. But there's a big piece of furniture blocking our way. Can you give us a hand?"

The architect gave a bow and passed through the wall into the other room. Vivi let out a yelp of surprise.

"Yeah, they do that," Benji said. "You'll get used to it. Sort of."

The group made their way into the office as Elijah positioned himself at the base of the stairs. He raised his hand, and the trapdoor shook weakly before coming to a sudden stop. A worried look passed over the ghost's face, as though the task before him was a lot more difficult than he had initially thought.

"Is it too heavy?" Benji asked.

"Maybe he's just tired," Vivi said. "Do ghosts get tired?"

"What's our plan B?" Benji asked.

"This was our plan B," Cordelia said. "Plan A was not getting caught, remember?"

"Oh yeah," Benji said. He turned to Cordelia with a hopeful grin. "Plan C?"

Elijah balled his fingers into fists, and the floorboards above him began to shake like storm doors during a tornado. Just a few seconds later, however, he dropped his arms and slumped forward. The floorboards stopped moving.

"This isn't working," Cordelia said.

"It doesn't matter," replied Agnes, picking through the burnt remains of Elijah's directions. "We don't know how to turn off the portal pyramids anyway. Even if we get out of here, there's no way to stop them."

"One step at a time," Cordelia said. "Maybe there's another way out of here. A secret passageway or something."

"You know how many hours we've spent in this office?" Benji asked. "If there was a secret passageway, we definitely would have found it by now!"

"I agree," Agnes said. "It's a waste of time."

"What kind of attitude is that?" Vivi asked. "We can't just give up!"

"Exactly," Cordelia said, sharing a quick smile with Vivi. "Agnes—you search the shelves to see if there's another copy of Elijah's directions. Benji and Vivi, you two—"

"Shh," Benji said, pointing up. "Listen."

There were footsteps above them. Someone was coming.

"Dunsworth's back," Cordelia whispered. Her mind scrambled, wondering what they should do. Hide? Fight?

What if they catch us? Whose body will Dunsworth make a home of?

Vivi? Agnes?

Me?

"Hey!" said a voice from above. "You kids down there?"

It was Darius Shadow.

"You came!" Benji yelled, jumping up and down. "You have to get us out of here! Can you move that armoire?"

Cordelia heard a few grunts of exertion as Darius gave it a shot.

"Sorry," he said, gasping for breath. "Too heavy."

"What if they work together?" Agnes said. "Darius pushes from up there while Elijah poltergeists from down here?"

Elijah gave a half-hearted nod. He didn't look very confident.

"Get ready to try again," Cordelia told Darius. "Only you're going to have a little help this time."

Elijah squeezed his eyes shut and clenched both fists. The floorboards shook, fiercer than ever. Cordelia heard the armoire buck up and down and waved her friends back, just in case it crashed through the floor. In the end, however, the floorboards held, and the armoire remained in place. The only evidence of their efforts was a crack that allowed Cordelia to see Darius looking down at them.

"How did the armoire just move?" he asked.

"Poltergeist," Cordelia said. "But the armoire's too heavy."

She thought about mentioning the fact that the poltergeist was Elijah Shadow, his great-grandfather, but that would require a long explanation, and they didn't have time. At any moment, the dehaunter might start freeing the ghosts.

"Weight isn't the problem," Darius said. "The problem is he can't see it. Poltergeists can only move things in their field of vison. He should come up here."

"He can't leave," Agnes said. "The office is his ghost zone."

Darius slowly lowered himself to his knees for a closer look through the hole. The brass key dangled from his neck.

"Office?" he asked. "What kind of office?"

Cordelia noticed Elijah gazing toward the hole with a look of intense longing. At first, Cordelia thought it was because he had heard his great-grandson's voice. But then he reached out his hand, and Cordelia realized exactly what he wanted.

"Mr. Shadow!" she exclaimed. "Give me the key around your neck!"

"My key? Why?"

"Just do it. Please!"

There must have been something truly desperate in Cordelia's voice, because Darius lowered the key through the hole without any further questions. It was the key to the first house that Elijah had ever built, an object so important that he had given it to the people he loved most in life.

Of course, Cordelia thought.

She grabbed the key and dropped it into Elijah's hand. A black triangle opened above him. Within the Bright, Cordelia saw a simple cottage sitting on the edge of a lake. In the front yard, a pretty woman tended to a colorful garden. *Hallie Shadow*, Cordelia thought. Elijah's beloved turned in their direction with a smile, then rose and wiped the dirt from her hands.

"At this point, I don't even want to ask," Vivi said.

Elijah rose into the air. For the first time, he looked at peace. Cordelia was tempted to just let him go. He deserved a happy ending.

But he can't have one, she thought sadly. *We can't do this without him.*

"Please, Mr. Shadow," she said as his feet rose over her head. "I hate to ask this, after all you've been through, but could you stay a little while longer? I know that in life you were a good man who wanted to make up for all the misery you caused. This is your chance, Mr. Shadow. Help us."

If Elijah heard her, he gave no indication at all. Within moments, he was standing face-to-face with his wife. As the portal began to close, he gazed into her eyes and gently touched her cheek.

Only then did he drop the Brightkey.

The moment the key struck the ground, Elijah was expelled from his Bright like a fallen angel. The triangle slammed shut and vanished.

"I'm sorry," Cordelia said.

Elijah looked away, his eyes brimming with tears, and rose through the ceiling; now that he had refused his Brightkey, he was no longer bound to his ghost zone. A few moments later, Cordelia heard the sound of the armoire sliding across the floor.

Benji yanked the lever, and the floor opened above them. They ran up the stairs to find Darius staring in astonishment at the armoire.

"How did my key do *that*?" he asked.

"Later," Cordelia said. "Right now, you and Vivi have to get down to the conservatory and free the teachers. They might be able to help."

"Nice to meet you," Vivi told Darius. "This is not a normal day for me."

Cordelia turned toward Agnes. "You have to shut

the portal pyramids down before the ghosts leave the school. I'm thinking the dumbwaiter entrance is a safer bet than—"

"How am I going to turn off the pyramids?" Agnes asked. "I don't have Elijah's instructions, remember?"

Cordelia grinned. "You don't need Elijah's instructions," she said. "You have *Elijah*. He'll show you what to do."

The architect gave Agnes a quick nod.

"Cool," Agnes said. "But even with his help, it's going to take some time."

"I know," Cordelia said. "That's why Benji and I are going to create a distraction."

"And how are we going to do that?" Benji asked, clearly afraid of the answer.

"Something I just thought of!" Cordelia said, smiling brightly. "And it's totally not dangerous and insane!"

Benji groaned into his hands. "We're going to die," he mumbled.

Cordelia looked around at her friends, both living and dead, and a feeling of warmth filled her body, like drinking hot cocoa after shoveling snow. She wished there was enough time to hug every one of them. But each second they stood there brought them closer to disaster.

"Good luck," she said—and took off.

23

Face-to-Face

The safest route to their destination would have been the secret passageway accessed through the third-floor storage room, but Ms. Dunsworth had locked that up months ago. They had no choice but to sneak all the way to the fourth floor, where the ghosts would be gathering in preparation for their pilgrimage to the outside world. From there, they could cut through Dr. Roqueni's apartment.

As far as plans went, it wasn't ideal.

Benji and Cordelia crept up the western stairwell while listening for the slightest noise. The school was silent. As was Benji, who hadn't said a word since

Cordelia explained how they were going to create their distraction.

"Who was president during the Mexican-American War?" Cordelia whispered. "It's really bugging me."

Benji put a finger to his lips.

"Sorry," Cordelia said. "I babble when I'm nervous."

"What's there to be nervous about?" Benji asked. "This is a completely flawless plan."

"I didn't hear you come up with a better one. We need a distraction. This is going to work."

"How can you be so sure? Because of some page Agnes showed us in an old journal?"

"It's not just that," Cordelia said. "If Ms. Dunsworth was trapped, it only makes sense that—"

The door above them slammed open, and a line of students spilled onto the stairwell with the jerky, unpracticed steps of living marionettes. Cordelia recognized a few familiar faces: Francesca Calvino, her normally inquisitive eyes sharpened to a single task; Grant Thompson, marching with borrowed purpose; and Mason James, who looked pretty much the same. Brows were narrowed in intense concentration as the ghosts struggled to maintain hold of their new hosts, slipping in and out like cowboys clinging to bucking bulls.

Ms. Dunsworth was right, Cordelia thought, cringing

at the grotesque procession. *It's harder to possess a child.*

A boy she didn't recognize began to turn in their direction. Benji yanked Cordelia out of sight just in time.

"We'll have to wait until they pass," he whispered.

Cordelia nodded. It would add precious minutes to their trip, but they didn't have any other choice. She just hoped that Agnes was making better time. By now, Cordelia figured, she should be in the passageway with the portal pyramids, working with Elijah to turn them off.

If no one saw them, Cordelia thought.

A door opened beneath them. Cordelia heard footsteps heading in their direction—a second procession of students, coming from the floor below them. She looked up. The first line had slowed to a trickle, but it hadn't stopped.

Benji and Cordelia were stuck in the middle.

"Quick," Benji said. "Blend in."

Trying to mimic the jerky manner of the ghosts as best they could, Benji and Cordelia joined the line just as Miranda Watkins came out the door. She looked them over, eyes narrowed with suspicion.

"Where have you two been?" she asked in a haughty tone. Her hands spasmed for a moment before settling on her hips.

"Had to pee," Benji said. "I forgot about that part. Been a while since I've been alive, you know?"

"Eww," Miranda said, walking off.

The hallway was packed with students slowly making their way toward the mirror gallery. For the most part, the ghosts walked in silence—Cordelia imagined that talking while walking was a nearly insurmountable challenge—but every so often a hushed voice shared its future plan: "I'm going to eat all the rocky road ice cream I want!" "I'm going to travel the world!" "I'm going to wear a seat belt this time!"

Limbs flailed; bodies rocked unpredictably from side to side. Cordelia and Benji were jostled apart. Within moments, she lost him in a sea of bodies that was toothpaste-squeezed from the narrow hallway into the spacious mirror gallery, where older students directed the new arrivals into queues that had formed in front of each mirror. Cordelia quickly found herself eighth in line behind a mirror lined with seashells. Its curtain, along with the curtains of all the other mirrors, had been torn away. Peeking around the long line of backs, she saw the reflection of the first student, a funhouse distortion that wavered and jumped like a television with bad reception.

"It is almost time, my friends," Ms. Dunsworth said. She was standing on the large, sturdy table from the teachers' room, which had been repurposed as a makeshift stage in the center of the hall. For a single, horrifying moment, Cordelia was directly in her line of sight, but then a tall boy took his place in line and blocked her from view. For the first time in her life, Cordelia was grateful she was small.

"I know that you are still growing accustomed to these vibrant new shells," Ms. Dunsworth said, "but I promise you that it will get easier. Practice makes perfect, as they say!"

A hand squeezed her arm. Benji. He held a finger to his lips and led her through the lines of students, who were too busy staring spellbound at Ms. Dunsworth to notice them. They passed out of the crowd and into the hallway on the opposite end of the mirror gallery, feeling more exposed than ever. Cordelia could see the stairway that led up to Dr. Roqueni's apartment, teasingly close.

"Where do you think you're going?" a tiny voice screamed.

The crowd of students parted to reveal the boy once known as Ezra, pointing triumphantly in their direction.

"Well done, Harold," Ms. Dunsworth said, clapping her hands. "Luke! Eric!" Two boys stepped forward. One of them was a mean-looking eighth grader who had once lit his report card on fire in the boys' bathroom. The other one was Mason. "Gather a few volunteers and search the school. If these two have escaped, it means their friends are out there as well."

The two boys cut through the crowd, eager to follow their orders.

"What about these two?" Harold asked, sneering at Benji and Cordelia.

"We have a few minutes," Ms. Dunsworth said, straightening her glasses. "Let's have a little competition." She faced the crowd. "Bring them to me, and you go through the mirror first!"

Cordelia and Benji, not waiting another moment, took off down the hall. They were immediately followed by a stampede of middle-schoolers. By the time they sped up the stairs toward the door to Dr. Roqueni's apartment, several members of the track team were on their heels.

Please be unlocked, Cordelia thought. *Please be unlocked.*

Benji grabbed the doorknob. Turned. Pushed.

It was locked.

"Move!" Cordelia exclaimed, jamming her hand into her pocket. She withdrew the spare key that Dr. Roqueni had given her and slid it into the lock. As Benji shoved a boy named Stu Collins into the crowd of approaching students, Cordelia backed into the apartment and pulled Benji in behind her. Working together, they managed to slam the door shut and turn the bolt.

Dozens of fists pounded against the door. Cordelia wasn't sure how long it would hold.

They sprinted through the apartment and crashed through the door at the end of the hallway. The houses remained atop their wooden pedestals as though nothing had changed since the summer day when it had all begun.

"We need to hurry," Cordelia said. "I'll start with the ones on the—"

"Cordelia," Benji said.

His voice, sharp with desperation, was an arrow in her heart. She spun around and screamed. Ms. Dunsworth—the real Ms. Dunsworth—stood behind Benji. There was nothing particularly evil, or even notable, about her appearance. She was a middle-aged woman in a drab housedress that Cordelia doubted had been stylish even when she was alive. Her grayish-blond hair was frizzy and unkempt. If Cordelia had passed her in the halls of Shadow School, she might have assumed her Brightkey was a brush.

"Let him go," Cordelia said.

Ms. Dunsworth clenched the back of Benji's neck. She moved her lips, and Benji spoke like a ventriloquist's dummy. The voice was his. The words and inflection were not.

"All that running around," Ms. Dunsworth/Benji said, "and all you've done is trap yourself in a dark attic with the ghost who wants to kill you."

"Stop using his voice!" Cordelia exclaimed, clapping her hands to her ears. "It isn't right!"

"Don't talk to me about what's *right*," Ms. Dunsworth said, moving deeper into the attic. Benji's feet shuffled forward to keep pace. "Do you know how I died? I choked on a piece of overcooked chicken. Alone. In my dining room. And then I spent the next fifty years watching family after family move into *my* house and enjoy their precious happy lives. How I longed to be them. With enough practice, I learned how to do it."

Cordelia backed deeper into the attic. She glanced over her shoulder and saw that Ms. Dunsworth's house, which she had last seen in the conservatory, had been returned to its original position on the pedestal. It was a little crooked.

"Let me ask you, Cordelia, since you're so keen on right and wrong—was it *right* that they got to live while I didn't? All because I didn't chew my meat carefully enough?"

"I'm sorry about what happened to you," Cordelia said. "It was a terrible accident. But that doesn't change anything. Life isn't meant for the dead. It's meant for the living."

For the third time, a terrible grinding noise shook the school. It was followed by a soft whirring, like a machine kicking into gear. Cordelia heard shouts of joy coming from the mirror gallery.

"You hear that?" Ms. Dunsworth asked. A sinister smile stretched across her face—and Benji's face as well. "That's the sound of our liberation. My people won't begin without me, so I really need to end this as quickly as possible. I suppose it will be easier if I have hands to wrap around your neck."

She vanished into Benji's body. After flexing her fingers, just to make sure they were prepared to carry out their gruesome task, Benji/Dunsworth took a few steps forward. Only then did she notice how close Cordelia was standing to her former home.

"*That's* your plan?" Dunsworth asked. "You were snooping around during one of our faculty meetings, weren't you? You saw how I punished those who failed me." Benji's eyes burned with a cold, merciless fury that left no doubt there was an imposter behind the wheel. "Do you hope to trap me, just like Elijah did all those years ago? *Do you think I'm stupid enough to go anywhere near that damned house?*"

"No," Cordelia said. "But I do think you're stupid

enough to follow me into a roomful of phantoms."

She turned to her left and shoved a house off its pedestal. Glass shattered, and a tall figure suddenly appeared. It had a windowpane for a head—its eyes, nose, and mouth like streaks of mud—and venetian-blind fingers that scraped the floor.

"You weren't the only ghost that Elijah captured in one of these traps," Cordelia said. "And when ghosts get old, they change. Sometimes they gain special powers, like you. But other times . . ."

Cordelia knocked the second house to the ground, releasing a small girl with horns who ran on all fours out the attic door. At the same time, the man with the windowpane head strode in Ms. Dunsworth's direction. She screamed once with Benji's voice, then fled his body and plunged through the floor. The man followed her. Cordelia resisted the urge to check on Benji and continued to destroy the houses, afraid that if she stopped for a single moment, her courage, already teetering, would abandon her completely. She tried not to look directly at what she was releasing—a cloaked figure weighed down with chains, a sad-looking dog with a triangular collar—praying that they would feel too indebted to their rescuer to harm her. Fortunately, these phantoms—or whatever they were—seemed eager to get as far away from their tiny prisons as quickly as possible, and paid Cordelia little heed as they ran/slithered/flew out of the room.

She heard screaming from downstairs. She hoped that was a good sign.

"What happened?" Benji asked, rising unsteadily to his feet. A glowing orb brushed passed him, leaking droplets of light, and he nearly fell again.

"Help me push the rest of them over!" Cordelia exclaimed.

Working together, they made short work of the remaining houses. It was Benji who pushed over the last one: a stone farmhouse. Moments after it hit the ground, a scarecrow materialized before them. It took a moment to bow in gratitude before skipping out the door.

Cordelia had hoped that these otherworldly creatures, trapped by Elijah Shadow, might scare the ghosts out of their human hosts, buying them a little more time. As she retraced her steps to the mirror gallery, however—and heard the chorus of screams awaiting her—Cordelia wondered if she had underestimated the whirlwind she had unleashed.

24

Mirrors

It was chaos.

Students and ghosts were running everywhere—
sometimes together, sometimes apart. Two creatures
that looked like tri-winged pterodactyls fluttered over-
head, occasionally picking off a ghost and tearing away
a layer, leaving them fainter than before. A white sheet
that kept changing its shape glided across the floor.
Even the more workaday spirits—a tall woman wearing
a red scarf, a little boy waving a sparkler—were making
their presence felt. Ghosts fled bodies like passengers
abandoning sinking ships, leaving students to wake in
a state of shock and confusion. Fortunately, Vivi and
Darius had done their job and freed the teachers from

the conservatory. Cordelia saw Ms. Jackson–the real Ms. Jackson–help a frightened girl to her feet, and Mr. Bruce carry a wounded boy to safety. And then, in a sight that did much to renew her flagging energy, Cordelia caught a glimpse of Mr. Derleth leading an entire group of fifth graders toward the east stairwell.

"The portals are working!" Benji exclaimed, tackling a boy with blond hair. "Don't let the ghosts escape!"

Cordelia looked around the room and saw, with horror, that the mirrors no longer cast reflections. Instead, each one showed a different location just beyond the walls of Shadow School: the playground, the basketball court, the front yard. The ghost wearing Francesca Calvino leaped straight through a mirror and into the parking lot. She giggled and ran away.

"No!" Cordelia screamed, wondering how many other ghosts had already escaped.

She turned to Benji, but he was no longer there. Scanning the mirror gallery, she saw him on the opposite end, running at full speed. His target was clear: Ms. Dunsworth, safely ensconced in Dr. Roqueni's body again, heading for the nearest portal. Cordelia took off after them as Benji tackled Ms. Dunsworth from behind. She kicked him away and got to her feet, limping toward the mirror. Cordelia ran as hard as she could, but there was no way to reach her in time. With both hands on the frame of the mirror, Ms. Dunsworth took a moment to fix Cordelia with a vicious smile of triumph.

Before she could take that final step to the outside world, the mirror turned black.

"What is this?" Ms. Dunsworth screamed, poking the surface. It rippled like water. "Bring it back! *Bring it back!*"

Cordelia saw a boy next to her fall forward as the ghost within him was yanked away. It was a man wearing a tool belt. He looked confused as he floated across the gallery to a nearby mirror, which cycled between a scenic mountain lodge and hockey game before settling on a workshop laid out with every tool imaginable. Cordelia heard the sound of sawing and saw the ghost smile.

He vanished into his Bright.

"Agnes did it," Cordelia said, staring in wonder as the mirrors around her began to reveal all manner of paradise: still and silent lakes without a whisper of a breeze, a thunderous ticker-tape parade marching down a city street, towering stacks of books surrounding a comfy chair, cartoon heroes fighting a monstrous dragon, a baby in a crib. The paradises were as varied and unique as the humans meant to inhabit them. And here they came! All around Cordelia, ghosts were being pulled toward the nearest available mirrors. Some went willingly, clapping their hands as the dehaunter pinned down their eternal home. Others struggled. It didn't matter. There was no escaping the mirrors' hold.

Cordelia saw Elijah pass across the room. He gave her a tiny bow before sailing into his wife's embrace.

"What have you done?" Ms. Dunsworth asked, spinning around in horror. Ghosts were being pulled from all over the school now, forming lines at each mirror. "All I wanted to do was live! You ruined *everything*!"

She charged at Cordelia with murderous rage in her eyes. Just before her outstretched hand could wrap itself around Cordelia's neck, however, Dr. Roqueni jerked forward, spitting Ms. Dunsworth out like an unwanted seed.

A piercing whistle filled the air.

The ghosts covered their ears and turned toward the source of the sound: the largest mirror in the room, its red curtain still untouched. The cylinder that rose from its frame began to puff black smoke, and the curtain was sucked inward until it broke free of its rod and drifted across a nightmarish city of dilapidated factories and sleek black skyscrapers. Smokestacks belched plumes of fire beneath a sunless sky, and a single whiff of sulfurous air nestled inside Cordelia's nostrils. In the distance, she saw something with more mouths than legs scale a smokestack. It snapped the red curtain from the sky with a forked tongue.

Ms. Dunsworth closed her eyes with grim acceptance. A gust of hot wind carried her home.

25

The Gift

Cordelia walked through the hallway, passing bulletin boards that had been papered with yellow, pink, and blue pastels. A few kids passed her, rushing for the buses that would take them home for spring break. She saw Francesca Calvino and gave her a wave, but Francesca didn't notice. Her head was down in a book.

She has no idea how lucky she is, Cordelia thought.

A total of four ghosts had escaped through the portals, stealing the bodies of Francesca, Steve Warner, Aaron O'Sullivan, and Lisa Hill. Fortunately, Mr. Derleth had quickly organized the teachers into a search party, and the missing students had been dragged, kicking and screaming, back to Shadow School—where the dehaunter had yanked the ghosts from their bodies. When the children awoke, none of them remembered what had happened.

Cordelia shifted her backpack and felt its contents move.

Ugh, she thought, wincing. *I hope I didn't mess them up.*

She took the stairs to the basement.

Since there were no longer any classrooms down there, the custodians didn't feel the need to clean the basement as often as the other floors. The floor was sticky, and several lightbulbs were in need of replacing. Cordelia spotted an impressive spiderweb stretching from one wall to another.

A ghost appeared directly in front of her.

Cordelia screamed, then laughed at herself for screaming. It was the first time that she had witnessed a ghost's arrival at Shadow School.

So that's how it works, she thought. *They just show up. Out of nowhere.*

The ghost was a man in his fifties wearing earbuds, jogging shorts, and a black T-shirt. There was a word written across his chest, but the letters were blurred.

"Hey there," Cordelia said.

The jogger jumped at her words. He looked rattled, like a boxer who had just taken a hard hit to the head.

"Take a deep breath," Cordelia said. "Or . . . not. Sorry. Anyway, the dehaunter will bring you to your Bright at any moment. Your run through heavenly woods or eternal marathon or whatever it is. I really don't get you joggers. But just hang in there."

As she passed the ghost and headed down the hall-way, Cordelia noticed that his left shoelace was missing.

Big deal, she thought. *The dehaunter will take care of him. You don't have to do a single thing. And do they really deserve your help, anyway? Remember what happened? It wasn't just Ms. Dunsworth who tried to steal a body.*

Cordelia glanced over her shoulder. The man had wrapped his arms around himself and begun to shiver, as though he was trapped in a blizzard without a coat.

It wasn't all of them, though, she thought. *And even if it was—can you blame them?*

She removed the shoelace from her sneaker and tossed it to the jogger.

"This is the last time!" she announced to anyone who might be listening. "For real!"

Cordelia didn't wait around to see if the jogger took his Brightkey or not. As she turned the corner, however, she glanced in his direction—purely by accident. The ghost was gone.

Cordelia smiled.

◆ ◆ ◆

Elijah's office had never looked so festive. Streamers hung from the ceiling, and multicolored lights decorated the shelves. A long table in the center of the room was covered with food and drinks. Agnes had made brownies, of course, but there were also organic granola bars, courtesy of Ezra's mom, and a seven-layer dip that Benji and Vivi had made together. A present about the size of a pencil box sat in the center of the table, wrapped with red paper and a gold bow.

I can't wait to see the expression on his face when he opens it, Cordelia thought.

She was relieved to find that her cupcakes had survived the journey in her backpack with their icing intact. She began to arrange them onto a paper plate.

"Those look awesome," Vivi said. "I can't wait to try them."

"Why wait?" Benji asked, reaching down to take one.

Vivi slapped his hand away. "No eating until the guest of honor arrives," she said.

"But I'm hungry. And all this food is right there, taunting me! It's cruel, Vivi! Cruel!"

"I think you'll survive," Vivi said, laughing as she leaned her head against his shoulder.

"I'm going to see what Agnes is up to," Cordelia said. Benji and Vivi had officially been dating for two weeks now. Cordelia was glad her friends seemed so happy together, but there were times when being around them made her feel a little awkward. Part of it, she had finally admitted to Agnes during a late-night FaceTime session, might just be jealousy. But it was more than that. Things were different now, and that was going to take some getting used to. She had always pictured the three of them—Cordelia, Benji, and Agnes—as an inseparable team who would spend their years at Shadow School rescuing ghosts. But now Benji had a Vivi. And the ghosts had a dehaunter.

It wasn't bad. It just wasn't how Cordelia had thought things would turn out.

At least we're still friends, she thought. *Ghosts or no ghosts, nothing will ever change that.*

She took a seat next to Agnes, who was watching Mr. Derleth and Ezra play chess. There weren't many white pieces left on the board. Ezra, wearing a tie and sweater vest, looked calm and collected. Mr. Derleth was sweating profusely.

"I'm guessing Ezra is black?" Cordelia asked.

Agnes nodded. "He's about to win his third game in a row," she said with admiration. "And the thing is—I've played Mr. Derleth in chess. He's *good*. He almost beat me once."

"So why don't you play Ezra?"

"Look at how happy he is," Agnes said. "If I beat him, it'll ruin everything."

"You're afraid he's going to win, aren't you?"

"No," Agnes said. "That's not it at all."

Cordelia raised her eyebrows.

"Okay, that's totally it," Agnes admitted.

"If you want, you can just play me instead," Cordelia said. "But let's play the type of chess with the round pieces instead."

"You mean checkers?"

Before Cordelia could respond, squeaky gears announced that the entrance to the office was opening again. Everyone stopped what they were doing and gathered around while Dr. Roqueni led Darius Shadow down the stairs. It was his first time in the office, and he looked a little overwhelmed.

"It's real," Darius said, eyes bulging. "I can't believe it. All of Elijah's research. His journals! His blueprints! The secrets of archimancy, all here!"

Dr. Roqueni gauged her uncle's reaction carefully. She seemed to be questioning her decision to bring him there.

"Thank you, Aria," he said. "Thank you, children! This is wonderful! We have to share this with the world, so people can finally know what a genius Elijah—"

260

"No," Dr. Roqueni said, shaking her head. "Absolutely not."

"But Aria—"

"The kids told me what you did, Uncle Darius. You saved their lives. You saved all our lives. Cordelia says I should give you a second chance."

"Smart girl, that Cordelia," Darius said, giving her a wink.

"She sure is. And I trust her. Which means maybe you can be my uncle again."

"I'd like that," Darius said. "More than anything."

"But there's one condition. You must swear to keep everything in this room a secret. If you can't do that, you need to leave right now and never come back."

Darius placed his hand over his heart. "I swear," he said. "I won't tell a soul anything about this place."

For a moment, Cordelia was certain that Dr. Roqueni was going to say she didn't believe him. Then she gave a weak smile and patted him on the arm.

"All right, then," Dr. Roqueni said. "Why don't you open your present?"

Cordelia grabbed the box off the table and handed it to Darius. He unwrapped it quickly and lifted the lid.

"Um," he said. "I don't mean to sound ungrateful, but this is an empty box."

Agnes laughed.

"They're spectercles," she said, reaching into the box and carefully lifting the invisible goggles. "They let you see the ghosts!"

"Like the glasses you were wearing when we first met," Benji said through a mouthful of cupcake, "only these actually work."

Agnes slid the spectercles over Darius's eyes, and he reached out to touch them, hands trembling. This particular pair had an old-fashioned, Steampunk look. Cordelia thought they made Darius look like the wise sage the heroes come to for advice in some sci-fi flick.

Darius tottered on his feet. Dr. Roqueni reached out and held his arm, steadying him.

"Give your eyes a second to adjust," Agnes said.

"The first time's the worst," added Vivi.

"I can really see ghosts with these?" Darius asked.

"As clearly as Elijah Shadow could," Dr. Roqueni said. "No Sight required."

Darius lifted the spectercles to wipe away his tears. Then he took a long look around the room.

"Well, where the heck are they?" he asked.

Everyone laughed.

"Come on, Mr. Shadow," Cordelia said, leading him up the stairs. "I'm sure we can find a ghost around here somewhere."

Spooky books by J. A. WHITE

> "A thrilling tale of magic that is just scary enough."
> —*Kirkus Reviews*

SHADOW SCHOOL

> "The suspense is engaging and consistent throughout, and there's a perfect mix of scares and mystery that will entice even the most fainthearted of readers."
> —*School Library Journal*